Marcus **nose**
against her cheek, used his fingertips
to draw circles on her back.

"I have a ton of activities planned, and a romantic evening at the château's spa that you'll never, *ever* forget."

His enthusiasm was contagious, and soon Simone was wearing a smile as wide as his. "I can't wait to leave," she confessed. "I just hope it isn't freezing cold there."

"Don't worry. I'll be there to warm you up."

"I look forward to it."

His eyes danced over her face, then crawled down her chest.

"All those extra training sessions with that reality star are really paying off," she purred, squeezing his biceps. "You've beefed up a lot these past few months."

His chest inflated with pride. "I love when you stroke my ego."

"And I love when you stroke *me*."

Marcus crushed his lips to her moist, lush mouth. His kiss scorched her, set every nerve ending in her body on fire. Swathing her hands around his neck, she stroked the back of his fine, smooth hair. Simone felt a hint of his tongue, and used hers to coax his out of his mouth. Their tongues touched and lapped, played and teased.

Nothing compared to kissing him, to being in his arms.

Books by Pamela Yaye

Harlequin Kimani Romance

Other People's Business
The Trouble with Luv'
Her Kind of Man
Love TKO
Games of the Heart
Love on the Rocks
Pleasure for Two
Promises We Make
Escape to Paradise
Evidence of Desire
Passion by the Book

PAMELA YAYE

has a bachelor's degree in Christian education. Her love for African-American fiction prompted her to pursue a career in writing romance. When she's not working on her latest novel, this busy wife, mother and teacher is watching basketball, cooking or planning her next vacation. Pamela lives in Alberta, Canada, with her gorgeous husband and adorable but mischievous son and daughter.

Passion
BY THE
BOOK

PAMELA YAYE

HARLEQUIN®
entertain, enrich, inspire™

This book (like all my books) is dedicated to my amazing parents, Daniel and Gwendolyn Odidison. Thank you for showing me what a loving, healthy, passionate relationship looks like. And for letting me read Harlequin romance books at a very young age!

ISBN-13: 978-0-373-86290-0

PASSION BY THE BOOK

Copyright © 2013 by Pamela Sadadi

Recycling programs for this product may not exist in your area.

Dear Reader,

Don't laugh, but I got the idea for *Passion by the Book* after watching a wild, raucous episode of my favorite daytime talk show. The guest—a lively young woman married a whopping six months—was desperate to put the "sizzle" back in her marriage and looking for ideas. Once I stopped laughing and wiped the tears from my eyes, I grabbed my trusty notebook and started feverishly plotting Simone and DeShawn Young's story. A story about two people deeply in love who unknowingly let the passion fizzle in their once-red-hot marriage.

I wrote this story for all the hardworking women out there who are juggling careers and family life (like Simone Young) and need an escape to a sensual, romantic world. I hope the suggestions in *Passion by the Book* rekindle the spark in your relationships. It did in mine!

I have a feeling that after you read the "drive-by" Simone did on her husband, you'll want to discuss it, and where a good church girl like me got the idea, so drop me a line at www.pamelayaye.com, pamelayaye@aol.com or send me a message on Facebook.

With love,

Pamela Yaye

Chapter 1

Simone Young saw her husband's silver Escalade roll to a stop on the driveway, and she leaped off the couch like a hurdler exploding out of the starting blocks. Chucking the September issue of *Vogue* on the coffee table, she flew down the hallway of her sprawling, five-bedroom Lincoln Park home, her arms swinging at her sides and her heeled bedroom slippers pounding violently against the hardwood floor. Seizing the lock, she yanked open the front door and planted herself in front of her husband like a living, breathing statue. "Marcus, where in the world have you been? I've been worried sick about you!"

"I can tell." Chuckling good-naturedly, Marcus Young patted his wife on the hips. "Baby, get back inside. It's freezing out here!"

The crisp Chicago wind sliced through her designer robe, chilling her legs to the bone. Stepping aside, Simone reluctantly allowed her husband to enter the foyer.

"I didn't expect you to still be up," he said, slipping off his polished leather shoes. "It's almost midnight. You're usually fast asleep by now."

The stench of sweat made Simone wrinkle her nose. "You stink."

"It's nothing a quick shower can't cure." Marcus wrapped his arms around her and lowered his mouth for a kiss. "Come here and give me some sugar."

Simone turned her face toward the wall. "Knock it off, Marcus. I'm not in the mood."

"Lighten up, babe. It's all good."

Oh, no, it's not! His blithe, carefree attitude aggravated her, and when he strode nonchalantly into their gourmet kitchen, opened the stainless steel fridge and grabbed a bottle of Vitaminwater, her frustration mounted. "Where have you been?" she repeated slowly, as if he was hard of hearing. "You said you'd be home in time for dinner."

"Lower your voice, baby. You'll wake the boys."

"Is it too much to ask for you to call when you're going to be late?"

Marcus broke the tab on his water bottle and leaned against the sleek, granite countertop. Hiding a self-incriminating grin, one that was sure to fan the flames, he tasted the cold, lemon-flavored drink. Despite the peeved, almost combative expression on his wife's face, she looked as pretty and as youthful as the day they'd met. It was hard to believe they'd been married for five years. It seemed like just yesterday he was chasing Simone down for her number. It was her staggering beauty that had caught his eye in that smoky, crowded nightclub, but it was her intelligence and wit that kept him coming back for more. And after discovering that she was pregnant—after dating for only six months—he'd gladly "put a ring on it." *I hit the jackpot the day I married Simone,* he thought, admiring her dark eyes, plum-thick lips that looked as sweet as they tasted and curves that made him drool like an old basset hound.

And she looks even sexier when she's mad, he thought, wetting his lips with his tongue. They were opposites in every sense of the word—he was a calm, laid-back type, while Simone was headstrong and impulsive, but Marcus felt their differences only heightened their chemistry. And seeing her riled up always made him hard. Turned on, he suppressed the urge to reach for her shapely body. She'd gained some weight over the summer, five, maybe ten pounds, which had gone straight to her hips. *All the more to hold,* he decided.

His mouth dried, and his heartbeat pounded in his ears like a jackhammer. He was trying to listen to what Simone was saying, but when her silk robe parted, revealing a wealth of cleavage, Marcus lost his focus. How was he supposed to concentrate when she looked so damn tempting in that short, virgin-white nightgown? The need to touch her was intense, overwhelming. But Marcus knew now was not the time to put the moves on his wife. Her hands were glued to her hips, and her stiff, unyielding stance told him he would be asking for trouble if he tried to kiss her again. But dammit if he didn't want to.

"Samson's closed hours ago, and I know you weren't working late because I called your office *twice* and there was no answer."

"My eight o'clock meeting ran longer than expected and—"

"Liar!" she accused, her thunderous voice tinged with disgust. "You weren't working late. You were probably at the bar with your stupid friends doing God knows what."

"You're right. I did go to All-Star, but that was after the meeting with my accountant." Marcus scratched at his neck. His skin felt itchy, like he'd spent the last hour rolling around in a bed of poison ivy. To get some relief, he loosened the knot on his tie.

Simone watched Marcus shrug off his jacket, and she couldn't help admiring how nicely his broad shoulders filled out his suit. All those years he'd spent training for various bodybuilding tournaments had given him a sculpted physique, and although he'd turned thirty-five over the summer, he had a better body than a college athlete. That's why he was paid substantially to train everyone from movie stars to chart-topping singers and entertainers.

Marcus was devastatingly handsome, and it didn't matter if he was wearing jeans, basketball shorts or a three-piece suit; he always looked fly as hell. He stood over six feet tall, had thick, perfectly groomed eyebrows and a smile that incited lustful thoughts in women of all ages. He was rugged, masculine, undeniably sexy with killer swag. *And a pain in the ass, too, sometimes,* Simone decided, crossing her arms.

"I took the staff at the new downtown center out for drinks," he explained, guzzling a mouthful of water. "I thought treating them to a beer would be a nice gesture on my part. You know, to show them that I'm not just the owner, but a part of the team."

Simone didn't want to stand in the way of her husband's career, but she wanted to see him for more than ten minutes a day. Their sons needed him, too. "You promised Jayden you'd set up his electric train set," she said, forcing herself to speak calmly. "He sat at the front window waiting for you, but you never showed. He's only five years old. How do you think that made him feel?"

"I'll make it up to Jayden this weekend. After I get his train set going, I'll take him to the mall and buy him whatever he wants."

"The kids don't need any more toys, Marcus. They just need you."

"Cut me a little slack. I'm trying my best."

"So am I!" Simone argued, her voice raising despite her attempt to keep it under control. "It isn't easy keeping on top of the chores *and* taking care of the boys alone, you know."

"Then ask the housekeeper to work a few more days a week. Better yet, make her full-time. You know that girl loves to bust some suds!"

Marcus chuckled at his own joke, but when he saw the terse expression on his wife's face, he stopped. Simone didn't laugh, didn't even crack a smile. He frowned, wondered what that was all about. She always laughed at his jokes, even the corny ones, and usually fired back a witty retort or two.

Marcus thought of telling Simone about his upcoming business trip to Manchester—the one he was hoping she'd accompany him on—but he sensed he should hold off. He'd tell her when she was in a better mood. Like tomorrow during breakfast, or the next time they cuddled in bed. With two kids, a demanding business and a large extended family, finding one-on-one time was rare, but he was going to make time this weekend to hang out with his wife. *Who knows?* Marcus thought, his gaze clinging to her soft, moist lips. *Maybe we can get started on baby number three.*

"I hate to see you stressed out, so if you need more help around here just ask the staffing agency to send over a maid." Pleased that he'd found a solution to her problem, he moved closer. He touched her cheek, stroked her flesh ever so softly. "Hire a nanny to help you with the boys, Simone. That will free you up to do more things in the afternoon. Like coming to see me at the office."

"I don't need a nanny, Marcus. I need *you* to help me raise the boys and spend quality time with us every day. Is that too much to ask?"

"No, of course not, but sometimes my schedule just doesn't allow it."

A shiver rippled through her, but Simone steeled herself against his caress. "Why can't you be home for dinner? Or take weekends off like everybody else?"

"I will, baby, as soon as the new gym is up and running to my satisfaction."

The look Simone gave him said she didn't believe him for a second. He knew he'd fed her that line when he showed up late for her cousin's wedding last month, and every time he canceled their dinner plans.

"I'm going to take a whole month off," he promised, winking at her as he put his arms around her waist. "I'll be around here so much you'll be begging me to go back to work!"

"You've said that so many times I've given up hope of it ever happening."

"Don't be like that…"

"Don't be like what?" she repeated, her eyes narrowed, her tone harsh as if her tongue was coated with the bitter, acrid film of resentment and anger. She wasn't backing down. "I'm sick of being a single parent. It's time you stepped up and became the man of the house."

He dropped his hands from around her waist. "Until I hire a suitable manager for the downtown location, I'm in charge. That means I'm the first one at Samson's and the last one to leave. What do you expect me to do when the women are dawdling in the changing room or the Michael Jordan wannabes ask for five more minutes on the court to perfect their jump shot? Tell them to get out because my wife's given me a nine-o'clock curfew?"

Simone gave him a look that could freeze hell. "This is not about me. It's about the boys. Jayden and Jordan are constantly asking me where you are, and I hate making up excuses for why you're not here with us—"

"Thanks, Simone, I can always count on you to make me feel like crap." Marcus crushed the water bottle and hurled it into the recycling bin. "I don't have the energy to argue with you. I had a long day, and all I want to do is take a shower and go to bed."

Anticipating his next move, Simone slid beside the stove, cutting off his intended escape route. Arms crossed, her furious scowl matching the smoke in her eyes, she spoke freely, without restraint. "All you care about is your business and hanging out with your asinine friends. You don't care about me or the kids or our family. We hardly see you anymore, and when you're here, you're on your cell or working in the office."

"What are you talking about? Everything I do is for you and the kids."

"Just admit it. You'd rather be out having fun with your staff than—"

"Having fun?" He barked a loud, harsh laugh. "Do you have any idea how crazy things are at the new downtown location? I'm so busy I have to schedule bathroom breaks."

Simone hated seeing the defeated expression on Marcus's face, hated herself for being the one who put it there. Taking a deep breath helped her regain control. Her husband didn't respond to threats, and although there was a lot more Simone wanted to say, she knew when it was time to back off. "Can you at least try to be home by dinner, so we can eat together as a family—"

"I'm going to bed." His words were clipped, his tone stiff. "Good night."

"Aren't you going to eat?"

"I'm not hungry."

"But I made chicken marsala." Simone opened the microwave, took out an overflowing dish and set it down on the granite countertop. "I made it just the way you like it, with tons of garlic, fresh basil and oregano."

"I had a steak burger at the bar."

Simone watched Marcus trudge out of the kitchen and up the winding staircase. On the second floor, she heard his steps slow, then stop, and knew he was checking on Jayden and Jordan. He did it every night, no matter how late he got home.

Simone stood there, as still as a mannequin in a department store window. She didn't know if it was arguing with Marcus or all the hours she had spent scrubbing the kitchen floors, but she could feel the beginnings of a headache. *What just happened?* she wondered, massaging her temples. *Marcus is the one who messed up, so why do I feel guilty?*

After putting the food in the fridge and turning off the lights, Simone checked on Jayden and Jordan. They looked so peaceful, asleep in their deluxe bunk beds, clutching their teddy bears. She stood in the doorway, watching her babies sleep, and felt such an overwhelming sense of love that tears pricked her eyes. It was hard to believe they were already in kindergarten. They were growing up so fast, learning so many new words and skills that she was struggling to keep up.

Seeing her sons lifted Simone's spirits, and as she walked down the hallway, past the den and the playroom, a smile warmed her lips. She had two beautiful children; a gorgeous, lavish home; and, for the first time in her life, financial security. And once Marcus stopped taking her for granted, and put their family first, she'd have the marriage she had always dreamed of.

Inside the master bedroom, the balcony doors were ajar, allowing the dazzling, crescent moon to light the colorful, cozy space. Marcus was perched on the edge of their custom-made bed in his boxer shorts, clutching his cell phone. He looked deep in thought, as if he was grappling with the answer to a trigonometry problem, but Simone knew he was only checking the day's football scores. "The couples seminar I mentioned to you last week is being held at the Regency on Saturday night," she said, "and I'd *really* appreciate it if you were on time. It starts at five o'clock."

Marcus rested his cell phone on the side table. "I'll try my best, but I have a session with that Persian fitness model on Saturday afternoon, and her workouts always tend to run long."

I bet they do. "Please be on time. This is important to me."

"Like I said, I'll try, but there's no telling when she'll show up."

"Then find someone else to train her and come home early."

Her suggestion was met with a yawn.

"I don't even know why you signed us up for that seminar. We're fine."

"We haven't been fine for a long time," Simone confessed, avoiding his gaze. "We argue constantly, and there's no intimacy in our relationship."

"What are you talking about? We were intimate a few days

ago." A mischievous expression crossed his face. "As I recall, you came *twice* that night."

Her lips parted, but no words came out. *He's joking, right?* Surely her husband knew the difference between sex and intimacy. But when Simone saw the proud, I'm-the-man grin stretched boldly across his mouth, she sighed. Apparently not.

Marcus must have read the bewildered expression on her face, must have seen the genuine confusion in her eyes, because he shrugged nonchalantly and said, "Whatever. Play dumb. But we both know you have no complaints in the bedroom."

Simone paused. It was true. They had an amazing sex life, and Marcus's kisses left her breathless. But French kisses and multiple orgasms couldn't fill the void she was feeling inside. Neither did weekly shopping sprees or sessions at her favorite day spa. She longed for more, for a deeper, emotional connection with her husband.

"Can't we just listen to one of Dr. Phil's audiobooks or something? I don't want to discuss our problems with a bunch of strangers. You know how people talk."

"This is a professional, highly acclaimed seminar, not one of your mom's weekly bitch sessions at your aunt Lorraine's house—" Simone stopped herself. But when she saw the harsh glint in Marcus's eyes she knew she'd crossed the proverbial line. "You have nothing to worry about. No one will ever know we went."

"Fine," he said, his mouth a firm, hard line. "If it will make you happy, I'll go."

"Great."

"Good."

Then Marcus stalked into the en suite bathroom and slammed the door so hard it rattled the balcony-door windows.

Chapter 2

Deep in thought, Simone plopped down on the king-size bed and kicked off her slippers. The pain of her husband's neglect weighed on her, felt so heavy on her chest she couldn't breathe. *If I wasn't so tired of having the same argument over and over again, I'd probably cry.*

Shoulders hunched in defeat, Simone stared down absently at her most treasured possession. She twisted her wedding ring around her finger, ran her thumb over the radiant, emerald-cut stone flanked by dozens of baguette diamonds. To the outside world, she and Marcus had all the trappings of success—money in the bank, a fleet of luxury cars, yearly vacations to exotic islands. They weren't keeping up with the Joneses; they *were* the Joneses. But ever since Marcus had opened a sixth Samson's Gym location she hardly saw him. All he cared about was building his brand. He was trying to become the Magic Johnson of the East Coast, and if the staggering sales of his first fitness DVD were any indication of his future, he was well on his way. Simone was proud of him, but she missed how close they used to be, how fun and passionate their relationship once was.

Things had been terse between them for weeks. They were cordial to each other, polite, but the tension in the house was suffocating. For days, he'd been moody and quiet, hardly his fun, jovial self. And since he wouldn't open up, Simone didn't know if he was stressed out about the business or as upset as she was about the state of their marriage.

"How did things come to this?" she wondered aloud.

Five years ago, Marcus had swept her off her feet. He'd call several times a day just to hear her voice, spent the entire weekend hanging out at her place and once played hooky from work so they could watch movies in bed. And when she was placed on strict bed rest in the last trimester of her pregnancy, and her mom couldn't travel up from North Carolina, Marcus took care of her. He brought her breakfast in bed, massaged her swollen feet and made so many late-night runs to Wendy's the staff knew him by name.

Simone gazed out the window, at the stars twinkling in the night sky, and thought about all the times she and Marcus had made love in the backyard. They used to be so in love, so happy, so completely and utterly devoted to each other. But these days it felt like they were living separate lives. Reviewing their heated exchange in her mind, Simone wondered if she was being too hard on Marcus. He was a good man— ambitious, sincere, affectionate. Or at least he used to be. Before fame and fortune came knocking.

Simone bit the inside of her cheek. She had to do something, had to find a way to make Marcus listen to her. But what? Her gaze fell across the framed pictures on the armoire and zeroed in on the one taken at the resort in the Dominican Republic.

Settling back against the quilted pillows, she allowed the memories of the night he proposed to soothe her troubled mind. It was the most romantic moment of her life. They'd had dinner by candlelight, danced to the tranquil sounds of the ocean waves, then made love under a curtain of twinkling stars. Marcus had been so tender that night, so sweet. He always got mushy during lovemaking and often joked that he could be talked into anything after an orgasm.

A smirk tickled her lips. *Of course there's something I can do!* Her conscience jabbed her, told her using seduction to manipulate her husband wasn't the answer, but Simone silenced her inner critic. *All I want is to spend some quality time with my man. Is that so bad?* Deciding it wasn't, she opened the side table and rummaged around. "All I need are some candles, a Sam Cooke CD and that edible massage oil Marcus loves so much!"

In seconds, the bed was covered with the supplies. Confident she could turn the night around, Simone whipped off her robe, shook her hair free from its ponytail and hustled over to the vanity table. She knew just what to do to get Marcus's attention, and when he was finished having his way, *she'd* have hers.

Inside the bathroom, Marcus trailed the electric razor along his jaw. He usually used this time to think about ways to boost membership at the club, but instead of strategizing he considered the accusations Simone had made. Did she really think that he was selfish? That he was putting his business above their family? He couldn't censor his thoughts, couldn't stop her words from circling his brain. Her insults tormented him, made it impossible for him to think of anything else. He'd given Simone everything a woman could want. Closets full of designer clothes, a hefty monthly allowance and more diamonds than a jeweler's wife probably owned.

Marcus stared at his reflection in the mirror, saw how tired and haggard he looked. If Simone wasn't in one of her moods he would have asked her to draw them a bath. When he held her in his arms all the cares of the world ceased to exist. It had been like that from the very beginning, since day one.

A grin overwhelmed his lips when he thought about the

night he had met Simone. He still remembered the exact moment he had spotted her. She was with her girlfriends, dancing on top of a speaker at a hip-hop concert, shaking her booty like it was nobody's business. Their attraction was instantaneous, intense, like two unstoppable forces colliding. He ditched his friends, she ditched hers and they spent the rest of the night making out in the VIP lounge. Afterward, he invited her back to his place for drinks. They made love twice that night, and Marcus was so enamored with Simone, he stopped hitting the clubs with his boys and started spending all of his free time with her. And when they weren't together, he was calling and texting her. Marcus unplugged the razor and dropped it in the drawer. After turning on the water, he stepped inside the shower stall and allowed the rising steam to alleviate the tension radiating through his body. He enjoyed reminiscing about those early days, before the kids, before they started bickering and fighting. The moment he'd met Simone he'd forgotten every other girl. Marcus had never fallen that hard or fast for someone, and he enjoyed every minute he spent with the sexy social worker from Chicago's South Side.

Soon, pleasing Simone became his number-one priority. She was the most beautiful woman God had ever created, the only woman for him, and Marcus didn't want to lose her to someone else. That's why he'd surprised her with a trip to the Dominican Republic for their six-month anniversary, and why he'd popped the question their first night there. Two days later, they were married at sunrise on Boca Chica beach. His friends had thought he was crazy for eloping, but Marcus was in love and anxious to start his life with Simone.

Turning off the water, he grabbed a towel from the metal bar and patted his skin dry. Marcus gave more thought to what Simone had said. Had he made a mistake opening another gym? Simone used to meet him at the door with a kiss, cook him meals that would impress the White House chef and give him a kick-ass rubdown at the end of a long day.

Then, he opened his sixth fitness center and the loving

stopped. So did her daily inquiries about the business. They stopped confiding in each other and started arguing more. Simone quit being his rock, his sounding board, the person he turned to when he needed sound advice. These days she cut him off whenever he mentioned Samson's, and she complained constantly about his schedule. She was right though. He *was* working insane hours. On a good day, he'd leave Samson's by six and not have to do paperwork in their home office, but that rarely happened.

That's why he'd met up with his staff at All-Star Sports Bar.

He needed to unwind, and, contrary to what Simone thought, there was nothing wrong with him hanging out with his staff. It was good clean fun, and joking around with his employees helped alleviate his frustrations and stress.

Sighing, he rubbed lotion along his arms and down his torso. Apologizing to Simone was the right thing to do, the *only* thing to do. Facing her was the easy part. Saying sorry was another issue altogether, he thought, shaking his head.

Marcus stood there, thinking. Tomorrow he'd make it up to Simone. He'd have his receptionist send her the biggest floral arrangement she'd ever seen. *That's sure to get me out of the doghouse and back into her good graces,* he decided, pulling on his T-shirt. *And if I play my cards right maybe she'll come with me to Manchester at the end of the month—*

Wrinkling his nose, he sniffed the fragrant scent perfuming the air. He smelled sandalwood, patchouli, vanilla. That could only mean one thing: Simone was burning incense. Egyptian musk was her feel-good fragrance and whenever she wanted to…

Dayum. Simone was in the mood.

Marcus scratched his head, shook the thought from his mind. No way. It couldn't be. She was pissed at him. He cracked open the door and peeked inside the bedroom. Soft music was playing, the lights were low and Simone was lying on the bed—naked. His eyes widened at the sight of her thick, curvy body, and his heart raced like a cheetah in the wild.

What the…? Talk about a quick turnaround! An hour ago, Simone was ready to throttle him, and now she was offering her gorgeous, delectable body for his pleasure.

His breathing was heavy, rapid. Even after all these years, Simone still had the power to take his breath away. He loved her more today than on their wedding day, and just the thought of touching her, of feeling her warm, supple flesh between his fingers made Marcus so hard he could knock over the magazine rack.

Grabbing his towel, he furiously wiped away the water trickling down his face. Simone looked relaxed, at ease, as if she was sunbathing on a nude beach. She'd freed her hair from that hideous ponytail, and now her lush, chocolate-brown locks were flowing over her shoulders, brushing lightly against her erect nipples. They'd been married for years, but every time he saw Simone naked, he was blown away. She had big, beautiful breasts; a pair of long, thick legs he loved to feel swathed around his waist; and an ass made for squeezing and stroking and kissing. But not tonight. Simone loved foreplay—lots and lots of foreplay, more than the entire cast of *Sex in the City*, and he didn't have the energy finding her G-spot required.

His eyes roamed over her figure, lingered between her legs. The sight of his wife—stretched out on the king-size bed like a *Maxim* cover girl model—made his pulse rise, as surely as the erection in his boxer shorts.

Marcus licked his lips.

Foreplay be damned.

He had to have her.

Now.

When the bathroom door swung open, Simone sucked in her stomach and prayed that the red mood lights concealed the extra weight she'd put on over the summer holidays. One too many plates of barbecue, and now she couldn't zip her favorite pair of skinny jeans! Simone was glad she'd married a man who loved her for who she was, not for her looks. Marcus didn't care how much she weighed or what size she was, but her meddling mother-in-law sure did. Gladys took every opportunity to get on her case, and whenever Simone saw her she wished she could take a chainsaw to the family tree.

"I hope this isn't a dream…"

At the sound of her husband's voice, Simone blinked. A soft moan escaped her lips. Transfixed by his sheer, masculine beauty, she watched as he strode confidently toward her. Simone couldn't take her eyes off him, couldn't stop staring at his hard, muscular body. She desired him, craved every square inch of him. His kiss, his touch, the long, thick erection standing between his legs.

He's one fine-ass man, she thought, twirling a lock of hair around her index finger. He was built like the Scorpion King—muscled, toned, a physique rippling with tone and definition—and he had more charisma than the leader of the free world. He had a tribal band tattoo around his right forearm, the twenty-third Psalm written in fine script on his left biceps and the word *perseverance* across his chest. His tattoos gave him a sexy edge, like a bad boy turned good. Marcus carried himself with class, like someone who'd been born with a silver spoon in his mouth, but he wasn't related to the Rockefellers or a card-carrying member of a Yale fraternity. He grew up in a violent, low-income neighborhood, but by sheer strength of mind he'd pulled himself out of the trenches of poverty and achieved all of his personal and professional goals.

"What took you so long to get out of the shower?" Simone spoke in a sultry tone, one intended to arouse, entice. "I've been waiting for you."

"I see. And. I. Like."

She held up a miniature bottle of massage oil. "You look like you could use a good rubdown, so come over here and let me work my magic on you."

"You don't have to tell me twice!"

Simone giggled, felt herself start to relax, to unwind. Marcus smelled good, looked even better and was wearing a sly grin. His eyes were ablaze with lust, so dark and penetrating, she shivered with excitement. The soft music created a romantic feel, a real chill vibe.

"You better lock the bedroom door."

"Good idea," he said, nodding. "We don't want Jayden wandering in like the last time."

"I know," Simone agreed. "I almost died when I heard him say my name."

They laughed together.

Simone drew air in and out of her lungs, cleared her mind of all worries and stress. She was going to rock her husband's world, and after, when they were wrapped up in each other's arms, she'd persuade him to trim his workload.

"Baby, I'm…" Marcus stopped speaking. He stood at the foot of the bed, quietly watching her for a long moment. "I'm sorry about tonight. I didn't mean to upset you."

Simone heard the sincerity in his tone, saw the truth in his eyes. "I'm sorry, too."

"Do you forgive me?"

She nodded, reached out and touched his hand.

Marcus covered her lips with his mouth, kissed her with such raw intensity and passion, she groaned his name. Electricity passed between them, then rushed through her like a thunderbolt. Marcus cradled her face in his hands, used his thumbs to stroke her earlobes, cheeks and neck. A tingle shot down her spine. Every part of her body—from her ears to her toes—came alive with her husband's touch. Simone was on fire, hot, so delirious with need and pleasure she was shaking. One kiss—one long, scrumptious kiss—was all it took to get her wet, and when Marcus cupped her breasts, she tossed her head back and moaned from deep within.

Rap music blared from behind them, startling them both.

Simone broke off the kiss, gestured to the nightstand. "Honey, turn off your cell."

"Just ignore it."

"If you don't answer the person will just keep calling."

"It's probably Nate. The Bears beat the Patriots, and he's pretty stoked about the win."

Simone rolled her eyes to the vaulted ceiling. She didn't know anything about football, and even less about its overpaid stars. But now that her best friend, Angela Kelly, had returned to Chicago, she had someone to hang out with while Marcus was cheering on the home team. Now she didn't have to sit around waiting for him to get home.

Marcus grabbed his cell phone. He wanted to spend the rest of the night making love to Simone, but when he read the text message from his friend and business partner, Nate Washington, he knew his plans would have to wait.

"What's wrong?" Simone snuggled against his shoulder. He was frowning, and his chin hung so low it was sitting on his chest. "Is there a problem at one of the gyms?"

"No, I have to write an article for *Bodybuilder's Magazine*, and it's due tomorrow. It's a major promotional opportunity, the biggest I've had since I opened Samson's," he said. "Thank God Nate reminded me or I would have blown the assignment."

"Yeah, thank God," Simone mumbled under her breath. She felt numb, paralyzed from the neck down, unable to move. Good thing, because she probably would have snatched Marcus's cell phone out of his hand and chucked it out the window.

"I better get started on it."

"Now? But we were about to make love."

"I know, but the article's due first thing tomorrow morning." Marcus pulled on a gray T-shirt and black sweatpants. "This is my first piece for the magazine, and if the readers like it, I could end up with my own monthly column. Cool, huh?"

All Simone could do was nod. What else could she do? Demand he come to bed and make love to her? *Oh, yeah, that's real romantic!*

"If it's not too much trouble could you proof it for me in the morning?"

Simone forced a smile onto her lips. "Yeah, sure. No problem."

"Thanks, baby. You're a lifesaver. I don't know what I'd do without you."

"How long will it take you to write the article?"

He shrugged. "Not long. I know what I want to write, it's just a matter of getting my thoughts down on paper."

But when he pecked her cheek and told her to get some rest, Simone knew her husband had no intention of returning anytime soon. Rolling onto her side, so he wouldn't see the pained expression on her face, she pulled the blanket up to her chin and sighed inwardly.

"Sleep well," he said, switching off the bedside lamp. "I'll see you in the morning."

Simone watched him leave, watched helplessly as he took her confidence and self-esteem with him. The room was dark, the night calm, and the scent of her husband's aftershave swirled in the air. Simone willed herself to relax, to go to bed, but her restless mind chased sleep away.

Lying there, she studied the numbers on the digital clock, watched as the seconds slipped into minutes. Simone felt alone, unloved, like a child whose parents forgot to pick her up from school. Only she wasn't a kid. She was a twenty-nine-year-old woman whose husband would rather work than make love to her. His rejection stung, burned like antiseptic doused on a bloody wound.

Resting her hands on her stomach, she blinked back the tears that filled her eyes. Having twins had taken a toll on her body, and it was times like this Simone wondered if Marcus was starting to lose interest in her sexually. She didn't have the tight, shapely figure she'd had when they first met, and nursing her sons had all but ruined her boobs. If not for her fear of going under the knife, she would have had a breast lift years ago.

Simone stared up at the ceiling, wondering, thinking, turning questions over in her mind. *What happened to the sweet, sensitive guy who used to think the world of me?* she thought sadly. Marcus had been emotionally AWOL for months, and whenever they talked, she could tell his thoughts were a million miles away. He complained that she hassled him too much, said that she was unappreciative of what he did for their family. Could it be true? Had her incessant nagging killed their romance? For months she'd been telling herself that he was just stressed about work, but deep down Simone knew it was something else.

Panting, her head spinning, her heart racing, she bolted upright. *Or maybe it isn't something else,* she thought, swallowing the lump of fear in her throat, *but someone else?*

Simone shook her head, booted the thought from her mind. Now she was just being silly. Marcus wasn't the cheating type. He was a workaholic, but at least he was a loyal one. Another thought struck, this one more terrifying than the last. The truth was staring her in the face, flashing like a fifty-foot neon billboard: Marcus wasn't in love with her. That's why he was working around the clock and why he was in his office now instead of in their marital bed.

Sweat drenched her skin, soaked the plush, thousand-thread-count sheets. Winded, as if she'd been kicked in the stomach, Simone struggled to breathe. As she sat there, shaking, listening to the wind whistling through the trees, the same question ran over and over again in her mind.

Can my marriage be saved or is it too late?

Chapter 3

"Ma'am, would you like another dirty martini?"

Ma'am? Simone stared openmouthed at the dark-haired waiter. *But I'm only twenty-nine!* Deciding he was just being polite and not trying to insult her, she nodded and rested her empty cocktail glass on his tray. "And if it's not too much trouble, could you bring us some more of your garlic cheese biscuits? They're so good I could eat the whole basket myself."

"You did!" Angela Kelly quipped, pointing a finger at her. "I only had one!"

They laughed.

"I can't believe how busy it is in here." Simone settled against the oriental-style cushions lined up along the booth. "It's a good thing you made reservations or we'd be stuck in the waiting area like everyone else."

"That wouldn't be so bad. That sexy pitcher who plays for the White Sox just swaggered in, and, girl, he's even more gorgeous in person!"

"Now I remember why you like it here so much. You can

stuff your face *and* get your daily celebrity fix all at the same time!"

Simone laughed, but she enjoyed having lunch at the Skyline Grill just as much as Angela did, and not just because it was located on a bustling, tree-lined street overrun with cafés, hotels and upscale boutiques. The crowd was chic, the service prompt and the atmosphere lively. Glass vases overflowing with marigolds brightened the tables, framed photographs of the rich and famous adorned the walls and pop music drifted in from the adjacent lounge. From her seat, Simone could see Jayden and Jordan darting around the playroom, and she smiled sympathetically at the waitress keeping watch over the roomful of rambunctious toddlers.

"I need a massage in the worst way," Angela said, rubbing her neck. "I interviewed a Saudi diplomat this morning, and every time I asked about the bribery charges against him, he cursed me in Arabic. I'm telling you, I earned my paycheck today and then some!"

Fair-skinned, with hazel eyes and an abundance of naturally curly hair, Angela looked the part of a confident, tenacious news reporter in her green military-style blazer, white blouse and slim pants. Her best friend complained constantly about her long work hours, but she loved interviewing prominent people—even the obnoxious ones—and was thrilled that she'd been hired to work at the number-one TV station in Chicago.

"Let's go to Destination Wellness tomorrow," she suggested, raising her cocktail glass to her glossy lips. "I'm telling you. That Euphoria Suite is calling my name!"

"I can't. I'm thinking of having some work done, and I have a consultation with—"

"You're doing more home renovations? But you just finished your deck."

"I'm not meeting a building contractor, silly. I'm meeting a plastic surgeon."

Angela's eyes were wide, glazed over with disbelief.

"I want to get a breast lift," Simone announced, pinching two fingers together. "And maybe a smidge of liposuction. I did some research on it this morning, and I can have both procedures done at the same time. Isn't that great?"

"Simone, you don't need a breast lift."

"Yes, I do! After nursing the boys my boobs became sort of, I don't know, squishy, and I even went down a cup size." Moving aside her salad bowl, she leaned forward and stuck out her chest. "Go on—touch them. See for yourself."

Angela looked like her chin was about to hit the table. "I'm not going to touch your boobs," she hissed, glancing around the dining room to see if anyone rich and fabulous was watching. "This is a classy restaurant, not some sleazy back-alley bar in the hood."

"Who cares? We've been friends forever, and besides, no one's paying us any mind. Go on, give them a good, hard squeeze."

"Forget it, Simone. I'm not going to feel you up in front of all these nice people."

"Some friend you are."

"You're insane for even considering having plastic surgery," Angela replied. "You're gorgeous. Stunning. Sexier than a video chick in black pleather booty shorts."

"I'm telling you my boobs just aren't as perky as they used to be."

"So what if they aren't? It's not the end of the world."

Simone gave her the evil eye. "We'll see if you're still singing that tune after you've had a couple kids and your body doesn't snap back like it's supposed to."

"You're starting to sound like that delusional Miami socialite I interviewed last year! What are you going to do next? Take some fat from your butt and inject it into your face to reverse the aging process?"

Angela's cheeky, off-the-cuff retort made Simone giggle, and when her friend threatened to send back the dirty martini the waiter brought, she laughed even harder. Simone lived for

"Girls' Day," and she loved every minute she spent with her childhood friend. Every Tuesday, they met for lunch, and over cocktails and ridiculously expensive appetizers they talked and laughed and ogled the hunky male celebrities dining an arm's length away.

"Where is all this coming from?" Angela's features were touched with concern. "You've never mentioned wanting to have plastic surgery before, so what's really going on?"

Simone fiddled with the napkins in the thin, gold holder. She'd cleaned up at the Neiman Marcus sale, scoring designer shoes and purses at fifty percent off, but she still felt miserable. Last week, she'd spent the entire lunch complaining about Marcus, but she'd promised herself she wouldn't discuss the problems in her marriage today. A lot of exciting things were happening in Angela's life, and she wanted to be supportive.

"I don't want to talk about it."

"Are you sure?"

Simone hesitated. She didn't want to burden Angela with her troubles, but if she didn't tell someone about what happened last night, she was going to burst. "It's Marcus…"

"Oh, no, what did he do this time? Fall asleep during pillow talk or after making love?"

"Ha, ha, you're so funny. You should open for Steve Harvey on his next comedy tour."

"Don't get mad." Angela winked. "I'm just being honest. You want nonstop romance, and that's just not realistic in this busy, fast-paced world we live in."

"Oh, shush. No one asked you."

Silence fell between them, but the dining room was alive with excitement and laughter.

"You can't expect Marcus to romance you 24/7, Simone. That stuff only happens on reality TV, and you're not on *The Bachelorette!*"

"I knew I shouldn't have said anything. You're single. You don't understand what it's like being married to a workaholic."

Angela put down her fork and studied her best friend. Simone always let her look reflect her mood, and her all-black ensemble suggested she had a serious case of the blahs. She'd pulled her hair back into a silver clip, wasn't wearing a stitch of makeup or her most prized possession—her big, glitzy wedding ring.

"I better go check on the boys. Jordan thinks he's a wrestler, and I don't want him trashing the playroom like the last time we were here."

"Sit down. The boys are fine." Angela reached out and squeezed Simone's hand. "I'm sorry, I didn't mean to be insensitive. Tell me what's going on. I'm listening."

Simone told Angela about their argument and about what *didn't* happen in the bedroom. "I tossed and turned for hours, and when I finally fell asleep I dreamt that we were in divorce court and that Judge Joe Brown was presiding over our case!" Simone shivered at the memory. "We were yelling and screaming and carrying on. It was ugly, girl. *Real* ugly. Worse than a *Real Housewives* reunion show!"

"Don't read too much into it. Marcus was probably tired and fell asleep in his office."

"Tired? Puh-leeze, what about me? I'm taking care of the kids and the house, without any help whatsoever from him, but you don't hear me complaining, do you?"

Angela started to speak, but when Simone glared at her, she swallowed her retort.

"I just want Marcus to spend more time with me. Is that too much to ask?"

Simone sighed, shifted around in her seat. Her gaze drifted to the playroom, and when she saw Jayden waving at her, she smiled and waved back. "Life was so much easier before Marcus opened his sixth gym. All he used to care about was making me happy and being a good father, and now all he cares about is tripling his net worth."

"Don't be so hard on him. At least he's not one of those lazy-can't-keep-a-job-can-I-hold-a-fifty-until-payday-type brothers."

Simone cracked up. "Don't worry, girl. You'll find your Prince Charming soon."

"Please, I've kissed so many frogs I've given up hope of ever meeting Mr. Right. Hell, at this point I'd settle for Mr. Maybe or Mr. Gainfully Employed!"

More shrieks and laughs.

"Angela, I'm so glad you moved back home. Now I won't feel so lonely."

"Lonely? What are you talking about? You have the boys, your family and tons of decorating projects to do around the house."

"I know, but I still get down sometimes." Simone shoved her fork absently around her plate of lobster pasta. "And now that Jayden and Jordan are going to the Webber Academy for Boys three days a week, I'm really climbing the wall."

"You should take a class or get a part-time job. That way, you have your own thing going on and you're not waiting around all day for Marcus to get home."

"I haven't worked for years, and the thought of revising my résumé makes me queasy," she confessed, her tone tinged with apprehension. "And to be honest, I don't know if I could juggle being a mom, a wife and a social worker all at the same time."

"Don't you miss working, though? No offense, but I never pegged you as a stay-at-home mom slash trophy wife type."

"That makes two of us. One day I'm getting ready to start my field experience at the teen clinic, and the next thing I know I'm pregnant with twins."

"I know, huh? It seems like just yesterday we were hitting the hottest clubs, staying out 'til dawn and dancing until our heels broke off, but it's been almost eight years since we graduated from U of C."

"We were going to travel the world after graduation, remember?" Simone wore a sad, wistful smile. "What happened to all of our plans?"

"You met Marcus and lost your ever-loving mind, that's what!"

"What can I say? My man has some *serious* game!"

The women giggled.

"But Marcus isn't romantic anymore, and the last time we went out for dinner his stupid cell phone kept ringing. I just want to hang out with my husband without anyone interrupting us."

"Have you told him that?"

"Only a million times," Simone grumbled, gripping the stem of her cocktail glass. "His favorite song used to be 'You're My Everything' and now it's 'My Prerogative.' Gosh, I always hated that song, and Bobby Brown, too!"

Angela laughed and dabbed at her mouth with a crisp, white napkin. "Every marriage goes through ups and downs, but that doesn't mean you guys are headed for divorce court, Simone. Marcus loves you just the way you are, so no more plastic-surgery talk, okay?"

Simone lowered her head and stared down at her French manicure. "I thought if I got a little work done he'd pay more attention to me."

"Getting a breast lift isn't going to cure your marital problems." Angela wore a soft smile, but her voice was stern. "Don't go to the consultation, or mention it to the girls on Saturday night, either. You know Tameika. She'll get loud and start talking crazy—"

"Saturday? Do we have plans?"

"My housewarming party's at six-thirty, remember?"

"With everything that's been going on, it slipped my mind."

"No worries," Angela said, with a dismissive wave of her hand. "You still have plenty of time to head to Nordstrom's and buy one of the fabulous items on my gift registry."

"You created a gift registry for your housewarming party?"

Angela grinned. "You bet your boots I did."

"Why?"

"Because I don't want my tacky relatives to buy me cheap dollar-store gifts!"

Simone belted out a laugh. She'd never heard of anything

so outrageous, but nothing her girlfriend did ever surprised her. Simone didn't want to miss the couple's seminar on Saturday, but she had to be at Angela's housewarming party. Her girlfriend had been planning it for weeks, and Simone was dying to see how she'd decorated her new two-story home.

"Mommy…"

Simone felt a tug on her sweater and turned around. Jayden was sucking his thumb with gusto, making loud, slurping sounds that attracted the attention of everyone seated nearby. Sniffling, he bobbed his head vigorously up and down. Breaking him of the habit had proven to be such a difficult task, she'd called his pediatrician for help. Dr. Westbrook told her not to worry, said that Jayden would grow out of it soon. Simone sure hoped so because she was tired of him slobbering all over himself, other people and the living room furniture.

"Mommy, Jordan called me a butthead!"

Simone inflected her voice with just the right amount of shock. "He did?"

"Uh-huh," he said, wiping the tears from his eyes. "And he said he's going to beat me up when we get home."

Angela ruffled Jayden's curly brown hair. "Don't worry, lil' man. Your brother isn't going to hurt you. He was just teasing."

"No, he wasn't." Another sniff. "Mommy, I don't want Jordan to be my brother anymore. He's mean, and he never shares his toys with me."

Simone pulled Jayden into her arms and kissed his cheek. He was five years old, but he had the temperament of an eighty-year-old man. He was moody and terribly sensitive, and when he didn't get his way, he'd mope into the living room, curl up on the couch and have a good cry. He did it so often Marcus had started to worry. Scared that his son would grow up "soft" and wanting to "toughen him up a bit," he had enrolled him in little league hockey. These days, Jayden cried more than ever.

"Mom, Jayden called me a butthead!" Jordan said, racing over to the booth. Sniffling, his lips curled into a pout, he mimicked his identical twin brother perfectly. "And he said he was going to beat me up when we get home!"

Simone strangled a laugh. Leave it to Jordan to make light of the situation. Lovable, energetic and as noisy as a boy could be, he lived to make everyone around him smile. To her husband's delight, he was naturally athletic, loved sports and enjoyed working with his hands. While Jayden was off drawing in his beloved sketchbook, Jordan was outside splashing in puddles, eating dirt and collecting bugs. "I want you boys to stop calling each other names." Simone watched Jordan, saw him stare down at his sneakers. "If you keep this up I won't take you to the video arcade later. Is that what you want? For me to cancel our plans?"

Jordan tugged at his sleeve, shuffled his size-three feet. "No."

"Well then, be nice to your brother."

After an extended bout of silence, he said in a low voice, "Okay, Mom. I'll try."

"That's my boy." Scolding Jordan pierced Simone's heart, but if she let his bad behavior slide, he wouldn't give Jayden a moment's peace, and the last thing she wanted was for him to spend the rest of the day crying. Simone knew all too well what it was like to be tormented by a sibling, and she didn't want her sweet, sensitive son to suffer the same fate.

"I'm hungry!" Jordan announced, rubbing his stomach. "Can I have some French fries?"

"No, you just had lunch."

"But, Mommy…" Jayden whined, joining forces with his brother. "My stomach's growling, too. I think it wants a cheeseburger."

Simone schooled her features, fought valiantly to keep a straight face. "I'm not ordering any more food, you two. It's time to go."

The waiter dropped off the bill and collected the empty plates.

"Where are you guys off to now?" Angela asked, signing the credit-card receipt.

"To buy you a housewarming gift, of course!"

"Good, then I won't keep you."

Simone hugged her. "Thanks for lunch. And the talk."

"No worries," Angela said with a flick of her right hand. "I'll see you on Saturday night, girlfriend. Don't be late!"

Chapter 4

Water Tower Place—a soaring, eight-level atrium teeming with designer stores, chic cafés and premier restaurants—was practically deserted, so after buying Angela the most expensive item on her five-page gift registry, Simone took Jayden and Jordan to their favorite stores. They played games at the video arcade, cuddled kittens in the pet shop and wandered around the bookstore perusing the discounted books in overflowing clearance bins.

"Mom, can we go to the kids' zone?"

Simone nodded and watched as they raced into the bright, kid-friendly area. It was filled with stuffed animals, oversize chairs and colorful tables. Staring outside the window, she marveled at the beauty of the azure-blue sky. The sun pushed through the clouds, spilling into the bookstore, lighting the wide, open space.

Warmed by the heat of the sun, Simone unzipped her winter jacket, and stuffed her leather gloves into her pocket. The bookstore was the place to be on a lazy winter day, and with seventy percent off already-reduced merchandise, it was packed with excited bargain shoppers. Mothers wheeled deluxe strollers through congested aisles, unruly children bounced off soaring book displays and the sleep-deprived students in the bookstore café guzzled coffee like it was holy water.

Simone took out her phone. There were no messages from Marcus, no texts. She'd called him after they left the Skyline Grill, but he still hadn't called her back. Simone didn't even know why she'd bothered phoning him. As usual, his cell had gone straight to voice mail. *Funny, he had no problem getting to his phone last night,* she thought, still ticked off at him for abandoning her in bed.

To kill time and to get her mind off Marcus, Simone strolled through the nonfiction section, checking out the bestselling books proudly displayed at the end of the aisle. *"A Sista's Guide to Seduction?"* Frowning, she rested her basket on the floor and picked up one of the pink, heart-shaped books. "How to seduce the man of your dreams in thirty days or less."

Simone let out a laugh. Normally, she wouldn't pay any mind to something so blatantly foolish, but in light of her present relationship woes, she decided it wouldn't hurt to take a quick peek inside. Thankfully, the display was only steps away from the kids' section, and she could keep an eye on the boys while she skimmed the pages of Dr. RaShondra Brown's latest book.

After a quick glance over her shoulder to ensure no one was watching, she cracked open the little pink book and flipped to the first page.

Have you lost your moxie?
Would your man rather hang out with his boys than give you the lovin' you deserve?
Are you tired of being ignored and ready to take matters into your own hands?

Yes! Yes! And yes! Simone thought, nodding her head. There were so many problems in her marriage she didn't know where to start. Who knew? Maybe Dr. RaShondra's book could make a difference. Maybe it could put the spark back in her five-year marriage.

Simone swallowed, loosened the knot in her silk scarf. Deep down, she knew that Marcus loved her, knew he only wanted the best for her, but the problem was he wasn't *in* love with her. His love lacked passion, desire, excitement, and that was precisely what Dr. RaShondra was peddling in her newest book. The good doctor guaranteed results in thirty days or less, and Simone was inclined to believe her. All six of Dr. RaShondra's previous books had skyrocketed up the *New York Times'* bestseller list and there was even talk of *Good Girl, Bad World* being made into a TV movie. She'd read the book in a day and had been the first one in line when the play opened in Chicago last summer. Dr. RaShondra knew her stuff, but that didn't mean the little pink book was going to produce miraculous results, did it?

Scanning the rest of the chapter, Simone wondered if Dr. RaShondra's self-help book was worth the thirty-nine dollars and ninety-nine cents. Ten easy steps to seducing your man and reigniting your relationship sounded like a scam if she had ever heard one. *But what do I have to lose? It's not like things could get any worse—*

"Simone, girl, get over here and give me a hug, you pretty heifer!"

Startled by the shrill, high-pitched sound, Simone flinched. Placing a hand on her chest didn't steady her raging heartbeat, and when Simone saw Tameika Brewster sashaying toward her in all her K-Mart glory, she groaned inwardly. *Oh, no, I spoke too soon!*

"You haven't been by the salon in weeks!" Tameika shrieked, her plump lips flared into a pout. "You're not cheating on me with a rival stylist, are you?"

Simone laughed and shook her head incredulously at the

brash Detroit native. Tameika had been her hairstylist for years, and even though she got off on teasing her, Simone considered her a good friend. Her hazel contacts were eye-catching, and so was her tight, leopard-print blouse. "I've been too busy to make it to the salon, but I'll stop in soon," Simone promised. "What are you doing here? Shouldn't you be at the salon doing something crazy to someone's hair?"

"I came down here to get a gift for Angela. Can you believe her crazy ass created a gift registry for her housewarming party?" Pointing a finger at her chest, she made a loud clicking sound with her teeth. "And you guys like to call me a diva. Ha! I'm not the only high-maintenance one in the group!"

The women laughed.

"I better round up the boys. I still have a few more errands to do today." Simone was about to return the little pink book to its rightful spot when Tameika ripped it out of her hands. *"A Sista's Guide to Seduction?"* Squealing, she tapped an acrylic nail on the glossy, heart-shaped cover. "Oohh, I heard this book was off the chain!"

Shooting her a be-quiet look, Simone retrieved her basket and smiled weakly at the slim, Asian man staring at them. Simone loved Tameika's zeal, her wild ride-or-die-chick vibe, but she was too damn loud for her own good. It was bad enough she was wearing an attention-grabbing outfit and a whole bottle of perfume, but did she have to talk loud enough for people in the parking lot to hear her, too?

Picking up her basket, which was weighed down with discounted books, magazines and stationery, she moved swiftly toward the beanbag chair Jayden and Jordan were sitting on.

"We discussed *A Sista's Guide to Seduction* at the salon just last night, and all the stylists and clients were raving about it!"

Simone slowed, in part to hear what Tameika was about to say and in the hopes that she'd decrease her volume. If there was one thing Simone hated, it was loud, obnoxious people chatting in quiet, confined spaces. The bookstore was not the place for Tameika to let herself go, and Simone prayed to God that her outspoken friend would keep her comments PG.

"You remember Peaches, right? That's the girl who did your hair when I was getting my boobs done." She patted her breasts, smiled prouder than a parent whose child was on the honor roll. "Well, Peaches said the book saved her marriage. Said Dwight was acting funny until she implemented the rules and quit waiting on him hand and foot. Now the man practically worships the ground her stilettos walk on."

Simone drew her eyebrows together. "Really?"

"Uh-huh, and my sister said the same thing. Her baby daddy has been helping out around the house, buying her gifts for no reason and spending more time at home, too."

"Seriously?"

"For real, sisterfriend. I ain't kiddin'!" she hollered, flicking her hair over her shoulders.

Closing her eyes, she envisioned Marcus greeting her at the door, kissing her passionately and sweeping her up into his arms. Simone shook the fantasy from her mind. *Right, like* that *would ever happen in this lifetime,* she thought, rolling her eyes. Marcus used to put her needs ahead of his own. Used to make time to do the things she wanted. Used to set aside time every day just for her. But over the past year, her needs had taken a backseat to his business, and Simone was sick of being ignored and neglected. Maybe she needed to stir things up a bit. Rock the boat. Remind him of just how spontaneous and fun she was.

"Buy the book, sisterfriend." Tameika tossed it into Simone's basket. "You need it."

Simone shook her head and raised her chin defiantly. "No, I don't." Okay, she did, but she didn't need Ms. Ghetto Fabulous pointing it out. And not in front of the group of women who had gathered around the pink book display.

"Oh, yes, you do," she countered, swiveling her neck. "You're forever complaining that Marcus doesn't pay attention to you, that he'd rather work or hang out with the guys than take you out, that he…"

Ouch. The heat that crawled up her neck burned her cheeks. *When did I say all that?* Simone wondered, trying to recall the last time she'd been at Glamour Girlz Beauty Salon. She vaguely remembered watching an episode of *Millionaire Matchmaker* and drinking a couple glasses of merlot while waiting in the reception lounge, but that was about it. *Next time, I'll lay off the wine and keep my big mouth shut.*

"*Dayum! Super* tall, *super* dark and *super* handsome at three o'clock."

"Where?"

Tameika motioned to the café. "Leather jacket. Rolex watch. Kenneth Cole shoes."

Simone shook her head, stunned at how acute her friend's eyesight was. Tamieka didn't miss anything. It didn't matter if it was a fifty-percent-off sign, a to-die-for man cruising down the street or a crumpled ten-dollar bill underneath a pile of leaves, she found it. The beautician had eyes like a lynx and the fearless personality to match.

"I'm lactose intolerant, but that's one tall glass of chocolate milk I'd like to taste…"

Simone followed her friend's gaze. The guy was cute, slim with dark eyes and skin, but he had nothing on Marcus. Not only did her husband have an A+ body; he had lips made for pleasing and a pair of long, slender hands that stroked her just right.

Shivering, she struck the thought from her mind before she got carried away. Back to Tameika's latest find. The guy looked responsible, smart, like the kind of brother who read the newspaper from front to back. He was just the type of man her wayward friend needed, but before Simone could offer her opinion, Tameika said, "I'm going to go talk to him. You don't mind, do you, sisterfriend?"

Simone gave her a hearty shove forward. "Take as long as

you need." *Hopefully, he'll keep her occupied long enough for me to grab the boys and escape through the side door.*

"I'll be right back," Tameika called over her shoulder, switching her wide, bountiful hips. One by one, men of all ages turned and stared. Simone couldn't blame them. Tameika did more than just flaunt what the good Lord gave her; she put the whole kit and caboodle on display. Her plunging V-neck blouse served up two cups of cleavage, her leggings clung to every curve and her outfit screamed, "Come and get me!" Thick, honey-blond hair flowed over her shoulders, and the more it swayed across her back, the more the men drooled. Tameika Brewster had it going on, and unfortunately for her next victim, she knew it.

Deciding she didn't need the little pink book and that it was a waste of good money, Simone dropped it in an abandoned shopping cart and slid into line. While she waited, she admired all the young, fashionable women flowing in and out of the store. *I haven't changed my look in years,* Simone thought, fingering the ends of her long, black hair. *It wouldn't hurt to do something different, something wild.* Coloring it a rich, vibrant hue like burgundy red was sure to catch Marcus's eye and give her a fresh, modern look. Simone loved the idea of shaking things up, but getting a breast lift was too drastic, and besides, her husband would never go for it.

Another thought sprang in her mind. *What in the world am I going to wear to Angela's party?* Just that morning she'd hunted around in her closet for something that looked good *and* fit right. It turned out to be forty-five minutes of pure torment. Her predilection for sweets had resulted in her gaining fifteen pounds over the summer, but dusting off the treadmill and eliminating junk food from her diet were at the top of her to-do list.

Opening her cell phone, Simone fully expected there to be a message or two from Marcus, and when she saw that her in-box was empty, her shoulders caved in. She'd called him ninety minutes ago, and he still hadn't returned her call. Simone sighed, released the pent-up frustration flowing through her. It was moments like this—when he was so busy he couldn't spare five minutes of his time to check in with her—that Simone had serious doubts about their future. How were they ever supposed to reconnect when all he cared about was his bottom line?

"Next in line please," the slender brunette chirped from behind the cash register.

Simone stepped forward, unloaded her books on the counter and returned the basket to its rightful place.

"Ma'am…"

Simone cringed and gripped her phone so tight she feared it would crumble in her hands. She was starting to hate that word. Twenty-nine wasn't old, and if one more person called her the *m*-word today she was going to lose it like a celebrity wife wielding a golf club.

"You spent a hundred dollars, so you're entitled to a free book," the clerk announced, smiling wide. "Why don't you take a few minutes to look around while I bag your purchases?"

Glancing over her shoulder to make sure no one was looking, Simone returned to the abandoned shopping cart, retrieved the little pink book and quickly slid it across the counter. "I'll just take this."

"Good choice. You'll love it. Dr. RaShondra is hilarious, and the rules actually work!"

"They do?"

The brunette nodded her head. "I've been married for eleven years, and my husband's never been more affectionate, so either the rules are working or he's having a midlife crisis. But either way, I'm happy!"

I would be, too, Simone thought, grabbing her bags and returning to the kids' section. "Come on, boys, it's time to go. It's getting late, and I still have to go home and make dinner."

"Awww, can't we stay a little longer?" Jayden asked, his

eyes glued to the talking book cradled in his hands. "I want to finish this story, Mommy. It's really good!"

"Ten more minutes, Jayden. That's it." Tired of standing, Simone dropped down in a cozy armchair and searched the café for Tameika. The stylist was nowhere to be found. Since the coast was clear, she opened the little pink book to chapter one and started reading.

A "Seductress" is a complete woman, a "Together Woman," a sister who knows who she is, what she wants and how to get it. A "Seductress" doesn't wait for things to happen; she makes them happen. She's on top of her game, savvy as hell and always well put together. She doesn't leave her house in tattered sweats or with jacked-up hair and stank breath, either. And since a "Seductress" knows her hair is her glory and her body's a temple, she doesn't skip workouts or forsake beauty appointments unless there's an emergency (think, death).

It's time to get it together, girl! While you work on getting your mind right, get your body right, too. First things first. Get rid of those funky flannel pajamas. If you look like his mother, he's going to treat you like his mother. Okay? Go all out when it's time for bed, too. I'm not telling you to don an evening gown, or drape yourself in diamonds, but for God's sake, take those damn rollers out of your hair and wash that exfoliating mask off your face! Sexify your wardrobe, girlfriend! It's time to burn the flannel and embrace the lace!

Simone hooted, cracked up until water filled her eyes. "Mommy, you're being too noisy."

Smiling sheepishly at her sons, who were staring at her with raised eyebrows and bunched-up noses, she said, "Sorry about that, boys. I forgot."

"It's okay," Jordan replied, reopening his comic book and settling back into his beanbag chair. "Just don't let it happen again."

For the second time in minutes, Simone laughed out loud.

Chapter 5

"How do I look?" Simone asked, exiting her walk-in closet. Jayden and Jordan were seated on her bed, a plastic bowl overflowing with fruit wedged between them. When she raised her voice, they glanced up from the cartoon they were watching on TV. "Is my outfit okay?"

"You look big, Mommy. Like a giant!"

Simone arched her shoulders and sucked in her stomach until it hurt to breathe. Standing in front of the full-length mirror, she carefully assessed her look. *Is it that obvious that I've put on weight? Shoot, if the boys noticed, surely everyone at the party will, too,* she thought, her eyes glued to her ever-widening backside. *Damn, Angela! I knew I should have gone for that free consultation at that cosmetic surgery clinic!*

"Mom's not big, Jayden, she's tall," Jordan said matter-of-factly, tossing an apple slice into his open mouth. "Mom's wearing girl shoes, and girl shoes always make her look taller."

Simone sighed in relief. Crisis averted. She'd spent the last hour searching for the perfect dress—one that highlighted her curves and hid her stubborn problem areas, but everything she tried on felt tighter than a straitjacket. After an exhaustive search, she'd decided to wear her favorite outfit—a slim-fitting chocolate-brown sweaterdress with capped sleeves. Pairing it with the swanky new booties she'd scored at the sale gave the dress a trendy, sexy vibe. Just like one of those blonde chicks on *Gossip Girl*. Gold accessories complemented her outfit nicely, as did her sleek, metallic clutch purse. A stroke of blush, a touch of lipstick and Simone was good to go. All she needed now was Marcus.

Where is he?

Simone glanced at her watch. It was five-thirty. The time they *should* have been leaving for Angela's housewarming party. She opened her purse and took out her cell phone. There were two text messages from Angela, but none from Marcus. Simone considered calling him, to find out exactly where he was, but decided against it. Dr. RaShondra said a "Seductress" didn't sweat the small stuff; she was cool, chill and never argued with her man over trivial things. Changing her attitude was going to take a lot of work, but Simone was willing to give it a try.

Simone put down her phone and picked up the little pink book instead. Two chapters in, and she was already in love with the book. And she was hopeful about her marriage, too. Dr. RaShondra knew her stuff and had a healthy fifteen-year marriage to prove it. The key principle of section one was simple. *Take care of your mind, your body and your soul. If you love you, he will, too.* Instead of waiting until next week to start eating right, Simone cleared the junk food out of the cupboards, cut her food portions in half and signed up for the Hot Yoga class at Samson's Gym. A few days in, and she'd already dropped three pounds. Sure, it was only water weight, but it was a start.

"Daddy! You're home!" Jayden and Jordan leaped off the bed and into their father's outstretched arms. "Yay!" they yelled with a loud cheer.

Simone smiled. Watching Marcus with Jayden and Jordan made her melt every time. He was so sweet with them, so affectionate and warm. They adored their father, and when he was home, nothing else mattered—including their beloved cartoons.

"How are you guys doing? Not giving your mother any trouble, I hope."

Jordan shook his head. "I was a good boy today, Dad. Just ask Mom!"

"That's what I like to hear. Anything fun and exciting happen today?"

The boys talked over each other, then laughed hysterically when their dad tickled them.

"Can we set up my train set now?" Jayden asked, his eyes deliriously wide and bright.

"Sure," Marcus said. "The last one to your room is a rotten egg!"

The boys jumped out of his arms and raced through the bedroom door.

"Marcus, you need to get ready for the party."

"It'll only take a few minutes to get the train set going."

"But it's almost six o'clock, and you know how Angela is about people being late." Simone put on her diamond earrings and secured the clasps. "She's already called here twice looking for us, and I don't want to get on her bad side tonight."

"It's not like we're going to a formal event," he pointed out, kicking off his sneakers. He unzipped his sweat suit, tossed it into the clothes hamper and selected a lightweight tan dress shirt from his armoire. "It's just dinner at Angela's, so what if we're a few minutes late?"

"Are you forgetting that…" At the sight of Marcus's naked body, her mouth dried and her heart raced. Simone blinked, forced herself to focus. "Are you forgetting that we still have to drop the boys off at the sitter's?"

"No need—my mom's coming here. I called her today, and

when I told her we were going out tonight, she volunteered to watch the boys. She should be here any minute."

Oh, so you have time to call Mommy Dearest, but not me. Simone strangled a groan. Gladys was as punctually challenged as her son, and although she set all the clocks in her house ten minutes early, she was always running late.

"Babe, where's the rest of the smoked turkey?" Marcus asked, slipping on a pair of dark tailored slacks. "I wanted to make a BLT, but I couldn't find the leftovers in the fridge."

"We'll eat at Angela's." Simone couldn't resist adding, "*If* we ever get there."

"Don't be like that," he said, staring intently at her. "I got here as fast as I could. I planned to leave the gym early, but my last client waltzed in twenty minutes late, then insisted on doing weight work at the end of his session. Damn reality stars!"

Simone kept her frown in place. Inclining her head to the right to get a good look at him, she brushed her bangs out of her face. His eyes were bright, and his lips were twitching at the corners. He didn't look sorry. In fact, it looked like he was trying hard not to laugh. "Is it too much to ask for you to be on time when we have plans?"

"I tried to leave work early, but it's just been one of those days. Today was the start of Samson's Fall Shape-Up Promotion and the reception area was so full I had to get some of the towel boys to lend a hand. By the time I finished up in the office, it was after five."

Simone wasn't moved. Marcus worked hard, and she appreciated the life he provided for her and the boys, but once—just once—she'd like him to show up on time. It wasn't often they went out without the kids, and when they did, they were usually the last couple to arrive. And that annoyed the hell out of her.

"Dad, hurry up!" Jordan hollered, poking his head out of his bedroom door. "We're patiently waiting for you!"

The couple laughed, shared a smile that caused the tension in the air to dissipate.

"I better go hook up that electric train before they flog me with the extension cord!"

"You have ten minutes, Marcus. That's it—" Frowning, Simone listened quietly for several seconds. She heard a door close, then the click clack of high heels on the hardwood floor.

"Grandma's here! And I brought McDonald's!"

The boys flew out of their bedroom, across the hall and down the stairs.

"Marcus, you forgot to lock the front door again."

He shook his head. "No, I didn't. Mom must have used her key."

"You gave her a set of our house keys? Why?"

"In case of an emergency."

"So, why is she using it now?"

"Because it's freezing outside and she didn't want to wait for us to open the door!" Marcus chuckled. "Relax, baby. It's all good."

Like hell it is! Simone clamped her mouth shut, swallowed the stinging retort on her lips. Channeling her inner Buddha, she breathed deeply through her nose and allowed the fragrant scent of fresh fruit to calm her. *A "Seductress" doesn't lose her cool every time life throws her a curveball,* Simone thought, turning back toward the dresser mirror to finish applying her mascara. *She handles every problem with poise, with grace, and knows how to pick her battles.*

"I'm going to grab something to eat while you get dressed."

"I *am* dressed."

"That's what you're wearing to the party?"

Simone stared at her dress, then back at Marcus. "Yeah, why? Don't I look okay?"

"Baby, please, you'd look good in a garbage bag…"

"But…" she prompted, sensing there was a lot more he wanted to say. "What is it?"

Marcus advanced into the room, came over to where Simone was standing. She smelled fresh, like a spring rain shower, and her scent aroused his desire. He slipped his hands around her waist, held her close. She felt soft and warm, and she fit perfectly into his arms. Simone was everything he wanted in a woman—no, more—and he took great pride in spoiling her, in buying her the very best that money could buy. And tonight he wanted to see her in something fabulous. Not a thick, bulky sweater that hid her drool-worthy figure. "Why don't you wear the dress I got you for your birthday? You know, the one with the ruffles."

Because it's butt-ugly, Simone thought but didn't say. Marcus, with the help of his young, fashion-obsessed receptionist, had picked out a short, strapless couture gown that had fortunately turned out to be two sizes too small. It was revealing, clingy in all the wrong places and looked like something that had been rejected on *Project Runway,* but instead of telling Marcus she hated the dress, she said, "I felt like wearing this. Is something wrong with that?"

"No," he replied with a shrug of his shoulders. "But you wear it all the time."

Her body stiffened. "Oh, really?"

"Yeah, you wore it to the fall concert at Mom's church, that art gala at the museum and..." Marcus saw her eyes narrow and trailed off into silence. To smooth things over, and turn her scowl into a smile, he tried to make her laugh. "Forget I said anything. You can wear whatever you want. I'm not the fashion police!"

"You're right, you're not," Simone snapped, crossing her arms. Marcus had some nerve criticizing her outfit. She always looked neat and tidy, and when she had the time she did her makeup, so why was Marcus acting like she was a slob? Okay, so she wasn't as fashion-conscious as she used to be, but it was hard keeping up with the latest trends when she had two rambunctious kids to chase after and a house to keep in order.

"Lighten up, baby. I didn't mean anything by it."

"Lighten up? I'll lighten up as soon as *you* start showing

up on time, remembering to call when *you're* running late and quit acting like the world rotates on *your* axle."

That felt good. But her satisfaction was short-lived. Guilt came, then a crushing dose of regret. *That's not how a Seductress behaves,* Simone thought, catching sight of the little pink book on the dresser. *A Seductress isn't high-strung or petty, and she never flies off the handle.*

Simone pushed out a breath, forced herself to think pleasant thoughts. Imagining herself at Destination Wellness, luxuriating in their plush Euphoria Suite, didn't help to calm her. Neither did the distant sound of Jordan's infectious, high-pitched laugh.

"Can we stop arguing long enough so I can share my good news?"

Turning around, she noticed the twinkle in his eyes and the wide smile playing on his lips. Marcus looked like he was about to burst. "What's going on?"

"A buddy of mine called this morning to tell me the Chicago Bears are looking for a new athletic director," he explained. "L.J. told the general manager all about Samson's Gym and gave him my business card."

"That's great, baby! You've been a Bears fan for as long as I've known you—"

"No, I've been a fan since I was in the womb!" Marcus chuckled good-naturedly.

"What exactly does the job entail?"

"I would create a detailed training regime for all the players, treat various ailments and injuries and of course attend all practices and games."

"That sounds like a lot of work."

"It is," he conceded with a nod of his head. "But I'm up for the challenge."

Her cheeks felt stiff, as if they were caked in cement, and her stomach was in knots. Simone was torn, troubled by her feelings. She wanted Marcus to be happy, wanted him to fulfill his lifelong dream of working with the Chicago Bears, but Simone hated the idea of him adding yet another project to his already-busy schedule.

"I have a meeting with Coach Tressel next Wednesday, and if things go well, I'll be one step closer to landing my dream job."

Simone squeezed his forearm and sent him a smile filled with love and warmth. She was going to be supportive even if it killed her. And when Simone thought about Marcus spending even more time away from her and the boys, she knew that it would. "I'm behind you a hundred percent," she lied, ignoring the bitter taste of dishonesty on her tongue. "The Chicago Bears couldn't ask for a more dedicated, hardworking man."

"Thanks for the vote of confidence, baby. It means the world to me."

Simone heard her cell phone ring and knew it was Angela. They were late for the party, and as usual, her best friend was calling to pinpoint their exact location. "I'm going to go change," Simone said, kicking off her shoes and tossing her metallic clutch purse on the bed, "I'd hate to embarrass you in my old, tired dress—"

"You could never embarrass me, Simone. You're intelligent and vivacious and you have the sexiest little laugh." Leaning in close, he glided his hands along her arms, down her waist and over her hips. "I just wish you showed off your body more. When you dress up for me it makes me feel proud, like I'm 'the man.'"

Simone straightened his shirt collar, then smoothed a hand over his broad shoulders. She inhaled his scent, allowed the tranquil fragrance to shower over her like a sprinkling of rain. He smelled like freshly brewed coffee, and he was every bit as strong and mouthwatering as the scent. Simone could stand there, in Marcus's arms, forever. Being with him was a natural high, the very best part of her day. These moments were rare, so few and far between, Simone couldn't remember the last time they'd held each other like this. Love spread through her, filled every chamber of her heart. "I wish we could stay home and cuddle in bed."

"Why can't we?"

"Because Angela would kill us!" Simone quipped, her eyes wide with fright. "Don't let her easy, breezy disposition fool you. Cross Angela Kelly and you're as good as dead!"

Chuckling, a wry smile on his lips, he wrapped his arms around her waist and slowly caressed her back. His lips grazed her neck, then brushed against her earlobes and cheeks. Kissing her, he drew her tongue into his mouth and feasted on the tip. His hands explored her soft flesh, filled her body with a delicious heat that caused her legs to tingle.

Simone tipped her head back, and when Marcus showered kisses down her neck, a deep-seated moan slipped from her mouth. He ran his hands through her hair, twirled the curls sweeping across her shoulders. Desire tore through every cell in her body. Aroused, her breasts swelled and her nipples hardened with pleasure. His touch excited her, and Simone loved how Marcus was making her feel inside.

"You feel so good, taste so sweet," he groaned. His voice was quiet, almost too soft to hear, but laced with lust. "I have to have you."

"We'll make love when we get home from the party."

"I can't wait that long."

"You'll survive," she teased, wearing a cheeky smile.

"Don't do this to me, baby. I've been thinking about making love to you all day." Marcus grabbed her butt, squeezed hard. "I'm going to smack it, flip it and rub it down!"

Simone giggled, then shrieked when he ground his erection against her and eagerly palmed her breasts. She wanted to remind Marcus that she'd been primed and ready to go the other night, but didn't. It was in the past, and she'd forgiven him. Or at least that's what she kept telling herself. "Baby, there's no time." Patting his chest, she leaned in and gave him a kiss on the cheek. "I need a minute to change, but if Angela calls tell her we're on our way—"

"What about a quickie?"

"A quickie?" she repeated, wrinkling her nose. "No way. Your mom's downstairs with the boys and I'd die if they overheard us."

"Then we'll do it in the bathroom, or the closet."

"How romantic." Simone wanted to make love, but a five-minute romp was out of the question. The en suite bathroom was spacious, filled with more flowers than a prizewinning rose garden, but getting busy on the sink just wasn't going to cut it. She wanted candles, music, her big, comfy bed, and some foreplay wouldn't hurt, either.

"You're not going to make me beg, are you?" Marcus took her earlobes between his fingers, stroked them, caressed them, applied the right amount of pressure to excite her. His mouth scorched her, moved so urgently and hungrily over her lips, her breath caught on a whimper. "You are so damn beautiful," he praised, whispering in her ear. "So sexy and desirable that I lose control every time you're around…"

Simone closed her eyes, murmured into his chest. Her ears were humming, her core throbbing, her legs shaking so hard she feared she'd drop straight to the floor. They clung to each other, like a couple lost at sea, and the scent of their desire was so thick it saturated the air.

"Marcus, honey, are you up there?"

At the sound of her mother-in-law's thin, breathy voice, Simone broke off the kiss and straightened her dress. Gladys had been raised in a poverty-stricken neighborhood, but she was as proper as the queen and hated public displays of affection. Sure, she and Marcus were in the privacy of their own home, but that wouldn't stop Gladys from scolding them. Or rather her. Marcus could do no wrong in his mother's eyes, and he wore the mama's-boy label with pride. "Hi, Gladys, how are you?" Simone greeted, pushing a hand through her tangled hair. "I hope Jayden and Jordan haven't been giving you any trouble."

"Never! Those two darlings are a joy."

Marcus chuckled. "I hope you're still singing that tune three hours from now!"

"The boys just need a firm, strong hand," she replied with a curt nod of her head. "I keep them on a short leash, but you two are softies. That's why they walk all over you."

Simone wanted to kick Gladys in the shin, but she projected calm. *Wouldn't Dr. RaShondra be proud!* she thought with a wry smile. "Thanks again for watching the boys, Gladys. We really appreciate it."

"You don't have to thank me for taking care of my grand-babies. It's my pleasure."

Simone felt Marcus's hand on her butt, squeezing, massaging, stroking it. Shivers overtook her, made her hungry for more of what he was offering. He moved closer, skillfully traced his fingertips along her thong. Simone glanced at him. He looked at her with wide-eyed innocence, like a kid caught with his hand in the cookie jar, and had the audacity to wink.

"Your cell phone's been ringing off the hook," Gladys said, addressing her son.

"I bet. I forgot it on the counter when I was rummaging around in the fridge for a snack."

"Yes, well, I noticed there was nothing to eat on the stove."

"I didn't cook because I knew we were going out tonight," Simone explained. "But there's plenty of leftovers in the fridge."

"Leftovers?" Gladys made a face that could scare the devil and his agents. "I certainly hope you're not feeding my son and those precious babies stale food. For optimal health, they should be eating fresh fruit and vegetables, not stuff that's been sitting in the fridge all week."

"I made the turkey Bolognese last night for dinner."

"Exactly! Who knows how many germs have grown on it since then," she chirped, her eyes touched with alarm. "I don't think I'll ever understand you modern women. I worked two full-time jobs *and* went to night school, but I still went home and made dinner every night."

But you're *the one who brought the boys McDonald's!* Simone bit the inside of her cheek to keep from speaking aloud. She wasn't going there with Gladys. Not tonight.

"I recognize that shirt," Gladys said, wearing a proud smile.

"You bought it for me for Father's Day." Marcus leveled a hand over his chest, a boyish grin on his lips. "I clean up pretty good, don't I?"

"I'd say. You look more and more like your father every day."

Simone's gaze strayed to the digital clock. It was time to go. Besides, once Gladys got started reminiscing, there was just no stopping her, and Simone didn't want to hear another convoluted story about her late husband. It was wrong to talk ill of the dead, but if what Marcus told her was true, the only exceptional thing about his father was the staggering number of jobs he'd been fired from. "Marcus, we better get going. It's almost seven o'clock."

"I hope you're not wearing that old standby frock to the party," Gladys said, her thin eyebrows crawling up her forehead. "You look—"

"Sexy and sophisticated," Marcus offered, slipping a hand around Simone's shoulder. "But that's no surprise. My baby always looks like a million bucks."

Simone cranked her head in Marcus's direction. He looked sincere, sounded earnest, as if he meant every word. Ten minutes ago he had wanted to burn her sweaterdress, and now he thought she was gorgeous. *What gives?* Frowning, she snatched her clutch purse off her bed and stuffed her cell phone inside. Simone wondered if Dr. RaShondra made home visits, because between Marcus and his mother she couldn't get a moment's peace.

"Mom, we should be home in a couple hours," Marcus said when they reached the bottom of the staircase. "But if you need anything just give me a call."

Simone started to give Gladys some final instructions, but when she saw Jordan and Jayden jumping on the couch, their ketchup-stained fingerprints on the living room furniture, a squeak tumbled out of her mouth. *I need a drink,* she decided, pivoting around and stalking out the front door. *No, better yet, make that a whole bottle of merlot!*

Chapter 6

Albany Park, a charming, working-class neighborhood with homes dating back to the Victorian era, wasn't a hotbed for criminal activity, but when Simone saw a group of teenage boys smoking in front of Angela's townhome, she felt a twinge of fear. Just yesterday, Angela had told her about a string of carjackings in the area, and Simone didn't want to fall victim to a brazen gangbanger looking to bolster his street cred. As a social worker, she knew all too well how deadly peer pressure could be, how lethal, so she suggested Marcus park on Twenty-Fifth Street. "There's always a ton of parking beside the nursing home," she said, pointing out the windshield.

"Oh, look, that car is pulling out." Marcus sped up the street, flicked on his indicator light and tapped his fingers impatiently on the steering wheel. "Come on, man. It doesn't take *that* long to put on your seat belt!"

Simone wanted to tell Marcus to find another spot, but after circling the block for the last fifteen minutes, she knew her husband was anxious to park. And eat. He was starving, and if not for her vehement protests, he would have stopped somewhere to buy a burger.

The neighborhood was filled with tall trees, a slew of charming, restored homes and the city's oldest park. The wind was bitterly cold, but the streets were crawling with college students looking to have some fun.

"I can smell Angela's cooking from here," Marcus said, resting a hand on the small of Simone's back and leading her up the brick steps.

A smile slid across Simone's lips. She loved when Marcus did that. The gesture, though small, made her feel safe, secure. Like he'd always be there for her. No matter what. It was a good feeling. *No,* she thought, leaning into his chest, *it is the best feeling in the world.*

"I hope Nate and the guys didn't finish all the grub."

Simone patted his chest. "Don't worry, baby. I'm sure there's plenty of food left."

She giggled when her husband frowned, but her stomach was coiled into a dozen knots. Simone had sent Angela a quick text, informing her that they'd be a few minutes late, but she knew her best friend was not going to handle their tardiness well. Aware of the prospects, she had come with a peace offering. Simone seriously doubted an expensive bottle of champagne would appease her best friend, but it was worth a try. Praying forgiveness was alive and well in Angela's heart, and that she loved the housewarming gift she'd had delivered that afternoon, Simone jabbed the buzzer and pushed away the heavy feeling in her heart.

When the front door swung open and Simone saw the fake smile plastered to Angela's lips, she knew it was going to be a long night.

"Look who *finally* decided to show up," Angela said, raising her eyebrows. "Didn't think I was seeing you tonight."

Marcus wore a sheepish smile. "Sorry we're late."

"You look fabulous by the way," Simone added, admiring

her friend's silk chiffon dress. "I love how your burgundy heels make the whole outfit pop."

"Uh-huh." Angela waved a hand in the air, then turned away. "Come in."

Cool jazz music mingled with laughter, conversation and the distant sound of the TV. The heavy aroma of barbecue chicken made Simone's mouth water, but she ignored her hunger pangs and admired the sleek, contemporary decor. Simone could almost fit the entire main floor into her master bath, but Angela had maximized every inch of space and created a trendy bachelorette pad.

Angela's recent trip to Belize to interview the country's first female president must have inspired her, because the main floor was brimming with color. Hints of turquoise—in the cushions, the area rug and the silk drapes—made the house seem bigger, wider. The glass, globe-shaped chandelier emitted a soft, spangled light, one that made Simone feel like she was standing outside underneath the stars. "Angela, I love what you've done to this place!" Simone praised as they stepped down into the living room. "It looks amazing!"

"I agree." Marcus whistled. "This place is tight, Angela. I helped you move in, but I hardly recognize it now!"

"Thanks." Her face was stiff, but there was a note of pride in her tone. "Maybe later I can show you the rest of the house."

"We'd love that." Simone glanced around and smiled sheepishly at the guests mingling in the living room. Kym and O'Neal were feeding each other hors d'oeuvres; Tameika and Dion were admiring the giant, black-and-white framed pictures on the wall; and Nate, Jameer and Emilio were watching basketball on the mounted flat-screen TV.

"Look who's here, everyone," Angela announced, with false enthusiasm. "It's Marcus and Simone, just in time for dessert and party games."

"Dessert?" Panic flickered in Marcus's eyes. "Does that mean all of the food is gone?"

Angela went into the dining room, picked up the knife on

the wooden cutting board and sliced into an apple pie topped with whipped cream and cherries. Fruit trays, cheese platters and an assortment of finger foods and drinks covered the long, rectangular table.

"Did you get my gift?"

Angela nodded, gestured with her head to the glass hutch standing along the far wall. "It arrived this morning. The personalized china bowls are lovely. Thanks."

"Are you going to stay mad at me all night?"

"I'm not mad."

"Yes, you are. I can tell. I'd be upset, too, if you showed up an hour late to my housewarming party." To smooth things over with her girlfriend, Simone did the only thing she could—blame her husband. "I was dressed and ready to go by five o'clock, but Marcus didn't get home until almost six. Don't be mad at me," she pleaded, wearing a sad face. "It's not my fault I unknowingly married a man who can't keep time."

Angela ran her tongue over her mouth as if she was trying not to laugh.

"Now, that we've cleared the air and everything's cool, let's get to what's really important here—your juicy, mouthwatering, taste-so-good-I'd-smack-my-mama ribs," Marcus said, eagerly rubbing his hands together. "You didn't let the guys eat my share, did you?"

Giggling, Simone stared wide-eyed at her pleading, begging husband. Marcus had a remarkable gift; he knew just what to say to soften a woman's heart, and his charms were working wonders on Angela. Her scowl was gone, and she was smiling like a pageant queen.

"Are you going to show me where you're hiding the ribs or do I have to rummage around in your fridge like a stray dog?"

Angela let out a laugh. Taking Marcus by the arm, she joked, "Come with me, Smooth Operator. I think I could find you a rib or two."

While Marcus went off in search of dinner, Simone fixed

herself a plate. Once she had selected all of her favorites, she went over to the sectional and sat down beside Dion.

"Hey, you," she greeted, making herself comfortable on the couch. Dion Houston was a shapely, statuesque, size-sixteen sister with a sunny disposition and the initials M.D. after her name. Simone didn't see Dion as much as she liked, but whenever they got together they had a blast. "How have you been?"

"Obviously not as good as you!" Dion inspected Simone from head to toe. "Girl, what have you been doing to yourself? You're looking all slim and trim and sexy!"

Simone beamed. "I still have a little baby weight to lose, so I've been eating better and working out. I'd rather eat a whole box of donuts than exercise, but you know what they say. A woman's gotta do what a woman's gotta do."

"Baby weight, huh? My son's nine, and I weigh more now than I did when I gave birth!" she quipped. "I'm just glad I finally met a man who loves me for me, because I'm not starving myself for anyone!"

The women laughed.

"Look at those two," Dion said, motioning with her head to Kym and O'Neal. "I don't mind couples showing a little love, but they've been going at it all night."

Simone gawked, looked on wide-eyed as O'Neal licked his wife's neck. "I've never seen them, so, well…"

"Amorous?" Dion offered, wrinkling her eyebrows. "If I didn't know better, I'd think Kym injected O'Neal with some kind of love potion or something because he doesn't have an affectionate bone in his body."

Simone agreed. "I've known them for years and I've never even seen them kiss."

"The last time I saw them they were on the verge of a divorce, and now they're sucking face like a bunch of middle-school kids in the bushes." Squinting, her face lined with confusion, she leaned forward in her seat. "I didn't believe Kym when she said *A Sista's Guide to Seduction* worked, but now I'm a believer!"

Noise erupted from across the room. Simone turned around to see what the commotion was and laughed when she saw Angela perched in front of the entertainment unit with her hands glued to her hips. A menacing glare wrinkled her face, and her lips were pursed together. She was arguing with the guys, and when her voice climbed to a fever pitch, Simone knew things were about to get ugly.

"What'd you do that for?" Nate Washington yelled, flailing his hands toward the flat-screen TV. "The game just went into overtime!"

Angela twirled her finger around in the air. "Whoop-tee-do."

"I don't expect you to understand. For excitement, you watch the news."

Munching on a stuffed bell pepper, Simone watched the heated exchange between Angela and Nate with growing fascination. Nate had to know that he was fighting a losing battle. Angela always got her way, and as soon as she batted those pretty hazel eyes, he'd fold like a house of cards. Nate had a gruff voice and a surly disposition, but he had a heart of gold. And he was so hot for Angela he was drooling like a bloodhound with a steak bone.

"We're going to play a party game," Angela said defiantly, her eyes slicing across his face. "I didn't invite you over here to watch TV, so grab some dessert and kindly join the rest of us in the sitting area."

Nate snatched the remote control out of Angela's hands and frantically hit the power button. "The only game I care about is this one, but don't worry, I'll join you guys as soon as the Celtics annihilate the Spurs."

"We are *not* going to spend the next three hours watching basketball, Nate."

"I never said you had to watch. Go 'head and play your little party game."

"Isn't spending quality time with your friends more important than watching a stupid ball game?" Angela challenged him with her eyes, dared him to contradict her.

"Whatever," he mumbled, flopping on the couch and folding his arms across his chest.

Victorious, Angela strolled over to the coffee table, picked up a white, rectangular box and waved it high in the air. "Great, now who's ready to play Intimate Questions?"

"Marcus, it's your turn," Angela announced, pointing at him. "Now, reach inside the box, pull out a card and answer the question truthfully."

Marcus shook his head. "No, thanks. I'll pass."

"Just pick a card and get on with it already," Nate grumbled, popping a cashew into his mouth. "Another game starts in ten minutes, and I'm not missing tip-off."

Tameika licked the icing off her fork. "Be a good sport, Marcus. It's all in good fun."

Yeah, right, until I put my foot in my mouth and Simone gets mad at me, he thought, grabbing his beer bottle and taking a long swig. *Why can't we play something safe like dominoes, Go Fish or a spirited game of charades?*

Marcus would rather have a prostate exam done live on the *Today Show* than subject himself to this silly, adolescent game, but since everyone was waiting expectantly, he reached inside the box and pulled out the first card he touched. Marcus hoped his selection wouldn't stir any controversy or start any mess. Easy, run-of-the-mill questions like, "Do you have any annoying habits?" or "What would you do with a million dollars?" kept the mood light and guaranteed laughs. Anything more challenging might get him in trouble, and he didn't want to upset Simone or earn a one-way ticket to the couch.

"Hand it over!" Wild with delight, Angela snatched the card out of his hand and read it aloud. "Do you feel it's important to tell your significant other everything?"

Marcus felt like doing the "running man." This was the kind of question he could answer correctly and score some points with, too. "Absolutely," he said firmly. "That's the cool thing about being married. You get a friend, a lover and a confidante all rolled into one."

A proud smile spread across Simone's juicy, pink lips.

Encouraged, he went on, "I don't confide in Simone because I feel obligated to. I confide in her because she's my best friend." He turned to Nate. "Sorry, man."

Everyone laughed.

"Simone's a great listener, she gives good advice and I value her opinion."

Marcus covered his wife's hand with his own. His feelings for Simone had grown tremendously over the years, and he loved everything about her—the sound of her girly, high-pitched laugh, how sexy she looked naked, the way she purred in her sleep. Simone was a terrific wife and an outstanding mother, and he felt proud to have her by his side *and* in his bed.

"I'm with Marcus," O'Neal announced, casting a protective arm around his wife's shoulder. "The biggest mistake a man can make is keeping secrets from his woman. The last thing I'd ever want to do is to hurt my Pooh Bear, so I make a conscious effort to always…"

What's up with O'Neal? Marcus wondered, scratching his head. Ever since the game started, the city bus driver had been gushing effusively about his wife. Marcus could understand a man wanting to win favor with his girl, hell, he'd been there a time or two before, but his weepy romantic gestures were over-the-top. To hear his buddy tell it, women were the salt of the earth and men were made to worship them. "Simone is the best thing that ever happened to me," he said, earnestly, truthfully. "She's got my back, and I know if I lost everything tomorrow, I'd still have her love and support."

On the surface, Simone kept it cool, composed, but inside she was a quivering mound of jelly. *Now, this is what I'm talking about!* she thought, sighing happily. *I've only read a couple chapters of* A Sista's Guide to Seduction, *but it's already producing results!*

"My wife and kids are my life," Marcus confessed. "And without them, I'm nothing."

"That's so sweet, baby. I feel the same way." Simone kissed his lips. "I love you."

"And I love you more."

I'm definitely getting some tonight, Marcus thought, squeezing her thigh. He couldn't wait to get home. Just the thought of making love to Simone made his heart race, pound, beat louder than a hundred tribal drums. His wife had lips made for pleasing, the flexibility of a belly dancer and hands that deserved to be enshrined on the Hollywood Walk of Fame—

"Quit lying, man." Still in a funk about missing the game, Nate grunted and shoved Marcus's shoulder. "You're supposed to be answering the questions truthfully not trying to sweet-talk your wife."

"Get out of here, man. I *am* telling the truth. I don't keep secrets from Simone."

"So you tell her everything?"

"That's what I said, didn't I?"

Mischief flickered in Nate's eyes. "Okay, Mr. I-Tell-My-Wife-Everything. Did you tell Simone about Miss December?"

Marcus shrugged a shoulder. "There's nothing to tell. She's just a client."

Always interested in a slice of fat, juicy gossip, Tameika turned to Nate and asked, "Who's Miss December?"

Nate bowed his head and closed his eyes as if he was about to recite the Lord's Prayer. "Carlita de la Cruz is the first Latina supermodel to ever be featured in the *Sports Illustrated* calendar, and does the girl ever have a body on her. Boobs, hips, booty, the works! And her mouth is so damn sexy I shiver every time she smiles at me."

"Stay focused," Tameika ordered, snapping her fingers in front of his face. "So, what does this Carlita de la Cruz chick have to do with Marcus?"

"I stepped to her with my A-game, pulled out all the stops, but do you think she cared? No! She was too busy flirting with this guy—" he thumbed a finger in Marcus's direction "—to notice me. She hopped up on the treadmill and served up a full cup of tits and ass. Had Marcus licking his lips like he'd never used lip balm a day in his life!"

Guests erupted in loud, raucous chuckles.

Marcus snuck a peek at Simone. She looked calm, composed even, but he sensed her unease. Her shoulders looked stiff, and she was twirling her wedding ring around her finger. *Great, one minute she's staring at me with love in her eyes, speaking in that slightly husky, wait-until-we-get-home voice, and now she's looking at me like I'm one of those trifling, cheating men on* Jerry Springer.

"It sounds like you're jealous," Angela said, raising an eyebrow.

"Hell, yeah, I'm jealous! Marcus gets mad play from his celebrity female clients and I'm stuck fighting off the buttugly girls! It's not fair!"

"What's not fair is having you as a best friend," Marcus shot back.

Laughter rippled around the room.

Simone clutched the stem of her cocktail glass. She didn't find anything funny about leggy calendar models throwing themselves at her husband. *No wonder he comes home late from work,* she thought sourly. *He's having so much fun at Samson's he can't remember to come home.*

"Come on, man. Keep it real." Emilio took a swig of his beer and rested the empty bottle down on the coffee table. "You're attracted to Carlita de la Cruz just like the rest of us guys."

"I'm not," he argued, tightening his hold around Simone's waist. "Carlita has an audition at the at the end of next month and she wants me to whip her body into shape—"

"I bet she does," Jameer added with a wink and a chuckle.

Simone tried to sit as still as possible. Everyone was staring at her, waiting for her to react, waiting for her to go off on Marcus like she had so many times before. But Simone wasn't going to lose her temper. There would be no angry glares, no hostile expressions, no snide remarks. Simone didn't like the sound of this Miss December woman, but she wasn't going to lose it on her husband—at least not here. "Flirting is harmless," she said, lying through her teeth. "It's good, clean, harmless fun, and just because you're attracted to someone else doesn't make you any less committed to your partner."

Marcus thought his eyes were going to pop out of his head. *When did Simone get so liberal?* he thought, shutting his gaping mouth. *Last week she almost pinched my arm off for chatting with a woman in the drugstore, and now she's preaching understanding?*

"Who wants more wine?" Angela asked, standing. "I still have several bottles of cabernet sauvignon and even some brandy…"

Everyone got up and went into the dining room to replenish their drinks. Marcus was glad to see their friends go. He wanted to assure Simone that his relationship with Carlita was strictly platonic, but before he could speak, she snuggled up to him and said, "I don't know what your schedule is like next week, but I'd love for us to have a nice quiet dinner alone."

"I think we need some one-on-one time, too," he agreed, leaning in close. "That's why I've planned a romantic weekend getaway for us."

"You have?"

His chest puffed up with pride. "I sure did, *and* Mom agreed to babysit Jayden and Jordan."

Simone blinked, waited for her husband's words to register. She couldn't believe what she was hearing. Marcus had planned a romantic trip for them *and* arranged child care? What the—

"You've been real stressed-out lately, and I wanted to do something special for you."

Openly staring at Marcus, excitement dancing along her spine, she returned his smile. He was stroking her hands ever so lightly, playing his fingers over her wrist, gazing at her intently. It had been ages since he had looked at her *that* way. Simone had no idea what Marcus had up his sleeve, but she was intrigued. Overjoyed, actually. This would be the first trip they went on without the boys, and the fact that it had come in the form of a surprise made Simone feel giddy with elation. "When do we leave?"

"That's for me to know, and you to find out."

"Where are we going?"

"It's a surprise."

Simone dropped her mouth to his ear, added a seductive purr to her tone. "Can you give me a hint? Or at least give me a clue about what the weather's like at our secret destination?"

"Sorry, no can do."

"How am I supposed to know what to pack if you don't tell me where we're going?"

"It doesn't matter what you bring—" his eyes caught fire, blazed with a smoldering, intoxicating passion "—because we won't be leaving our suite."

Chapter 7

"Faster, baby, faster!" Simone yelled, cupping her hands around her mouth and leaning against the glass that separated the rink from the bleachers. "That's it, Jordan! You can do it! Shoot!"

As Jordan reached the hockey net, he lost his footing, and slid facedown on the ice. Simone surged to her feet, stared intently at the spot where her son lay. Seconds later, Jordan popped up, adjusted his knee pads and set off, once again in pursuit of the puck.

Simone wore a wry smile. Typical Jordan. Sitting, she picked up her cup and sipped her hot chocolate. Her gaze circled the rink and fell on Jayden. He looked miserable—hobbling around with teary eyes and a runny nose and his shoulders hunched in despair.

Sighing, she shifted around on the stiff, wooden bench trying to find a comfortable spot. Simone checked her watch, wondering how many more practice drills the kids would have to do before calling it a day. Hockey was just one sport she couldn't get into. Players were allowed to duke it out on the rink, and when they weren't beating each other up, they chased around a puck. How exciting! That's why when Marcus suggested enrolling the boys in little league hockey, she'd refused. Simone didn't want her sons fighting. Or hitting. Or walking around with missing teeth. But Marcus assured her the emphasis of the sessions was on skating, and she gave in. He promised to drive them to and from practice and agreed to wash their smelly gear, too. It would be an activity the boys did with their father. Male bonding at its best. The boys would play, Marcus would supervise and Simone would have some "me time" every Monday and Thursday. Or so she thought. If she'd known that she'd be the one to drive the boys to Skater Zone Rink two weeks in a row, she would have nixed the plan.

I can't be too angry with Marcus, she decided, stretching her legs across the bench in front of her. *It's not his fault his assistant manager is out sick.*

Settling back into her seat, she cracked open Dr. RaShondra's book and started reading.

A Seductress knows that to get love, she has to give love. And the same principle is true of romance. When was the last time you gave your man a back rub? Or took him out for a candlelit dinner? Complacency is a romance killer, so do all those things you did in the beginning to catch his eye. Wear sexy lingerie. Spray the sheets with perfume. Trade those hideous bunny slippers for a pair of leopard-print stilettos! Meow...

"Mommy!"

Simone's head snapped up at the sound of Jayden's ear-splitting wail. He tried to skate over to her bench, but after falling, he got down on his hands and knees and crawled like a baby. Simone refrained from jumping up and racing over to him. Marcus said she babied him too much, said that she was raising him to be weak. Simone had to admit it; she did have a tendency to coddle him, but that's what every good mother did, right?

Calmly exiting the bleachers, Simone stepped out onto the ice and helped Jayden to his feet. Careful not to collide with the other children who were doing laps around the rink, she led him over to the penalty box, sat him down on her lap and hugged him to her chest.

"Honey, what's wrong?" she asked, wiping the tears splashing onto his hockey jersey.

"I hate hockey!" Jayden chucked his stick on the floor. "I don't want to play anymore. I want to go home!"

"Jayden, no one expects you to be the best skater. You're still learning." Simone caught sight of Jordan whizzing by and was impressed to see him skating easily. Aside from a few stumbles here and there, most of the children seemed to have the hang of it. The mother in her wanted to tell Jayden he didn't have to play, that he could sit in the stands with her until practice ended, but the social worker in her said, "Don't give up, Jayden. You can do it. I know you can."

Jayden whimpered like a day-old puppy. "B-but, I don't feel good, Mommy. My tummy hurts!" He grabbed his stomach and doubled over. "I'm sick!"

"That's funny, you were feeling fine five minutes ago." Simone cupped his chin and stared intently at his round, brown face. Apart from the tear streaks and the runny nose, he looked perfectly healthy. To make him feel better, Simone hummed the theme music from his favorite TV show and rubbed his stomach. "Ready to get back out there?"

"No. My stomach still hurts."

Simone heard her cell phone ring, but she made no move to answer it. In the last week, she had applied for several part-time jobs, and her phone had been ringing incessantly all day. But now was not the time to answer questions about her work history or schedule interviews. She had to get Jayden out of the bleachers and back onto the ice. "If you're sick then you'll have to spend the rest of the day in bed." Shaking her head sadly, she shifted Jayden off of her lap and onto the bench. "And that's too bad, because I was going to take you to the museum this afternoon."

"You were?"

"Uh-huh. Today's the last day of the *Charlie and the Chocolate Factory* exhibit, and I thought you'd like to check it out." Simone lowered her mouth to his ear and whispered, "I heard they have chocolate to eat *and* paint with. Doesn't that sound like fun?"

After a brief pause, Jayden wobbled to his feet. "My stomach is starting to feel better."

"So, you want to go back out there and play?" she asked, caressing his cheek.

Jayden nodded.

Simone watched him teeter back onto the ice. When he glanced over his shoulder, she waved. "That's it, honey! You can do it!"

Once Jayden was safely back on the ice and skating alongside Jordan, Simone took out her cell phone. A new text message from Marcus popped up on the screen.

Just wanted you to know I'm thinking about you.

A tingle fluttered through her body. This was the second message Marcus had sent today, and it was only ten o'clock! Smiling so wide her jaw ached, she sent him a short, titillating message sure to rev his engines. Since Angela's housewarming party, she'd made a concerted effort not to argue with Marcus. When he let Jordan eat ice cream in bed and he spilled the bowl on his blanket, Simone swallowed a curse and calmly stripped the sheets. And last night when Marcus fell asleep during Angela's segment on *Eye on Chicago,* Simone didn't elbow him in the ribs to wake him up. It was tough biting her tongue instead of speaking her mind, but Dr. RaShondra's rules were working, and things were starting to improve at home. She was sleeping better, arguing less with the kids and laughing more with Marcus.

Crossing her legs, she pulled her sweater tightly around her shoulders and buried her face in the soft material. Marcus's flirty text message made her feel all warm and tingly inside, but the rink was freezing cold. Simone felt like she was sitting inside a freezer, and her arms and legs were numb. Staring outside the window confirmed her worst fears. Five inches of snow had been dumped on the city overnight, and the white stuff was still raining down from the sky. Snow covered the trees and the sidewalks, and sheets of ice clung to the already slippery roads.

I can't wait for our romantic weekend getaway, Simone thought, rubbing her chilled hands together. *This time next month I'll be somewhere warm and exotic!* Their trip was still a week away, but she was so anxious to leave, she'd packed her bags and put them beside the garage door. Simone only wished she knew where they were going. Marcus was being as secretive as a Russian spy, and it didn't matter how much she begged or pleaded, he still wouldn't fess up. Visions of kissing under the vast Miami sky or strolling hand in hand along a white, sandy Caribbean beach played in her mind like a cherished home video. Simone told herself it didn't matter where they were going, but it did. She wanted to go somewhere romantic, somewhere exciting and exclusive. That way, she wouldn't have to worry about rowdy college students stumbling into them or any leggy model types pushing up on her man.

To keep from stressing over the details of their upcoming trip, Simone picked back up the little pink book and resumed reading chapter five.

> *Do a drive-by on your man once a week. That's right, I said it. Swing by his job, indulge in some heavy petting and then skedaddle. He'll be so hot for you, so turned on by that midday romp, he won't be able to*

*think about anything but you. So, don't be surprised if
your man comes home early from work to finish what
you started...*

Simone paused. *Did I just read that right?* Going to Samson's Gym for the sole purpose of seducing Marcus was brazen, reckless, like something a character in an erotic movie
would do. But the thought of doing it excited Simone. And
pouncing on her husband in the middle of his workday was
sure to get his attention.

Simone checked her watch. She wanted to go home and
change, but if she drove back across town she'd get stuck in
midday traffic. Besides, it wasn't about her look; it was about
how she was feeling inside. And reading chapter five had put
her in a sexy state of mind. Simone couldn't wait to see the
look on Marcus's face when she sashayed into his office, threw
her arms around him and kissed him passionately. She didn't
know if she could do something that bold, but when doubt
seeped in, she reread the last paragraph of the chapter and allowed Dr. RaShondra's words to imbue her with confidence.

*A Seductress doesn't waste time fretting and stressing.
She pours her time and energy into being the most fabulous woman she can be. And if you're the shy, timid,
Mary Poppins type just fake it. Hey, if Beyoncé can have
an alter ego, so can you! Hold your head up, tilt your
chin and throw your shoulders back because you're one
bad mama jama. That man you desire is yours for the
taking, so unleash your inner seductress on him and
don't hold back. And after you've rocked his world—
take a moment to catch your breath—and do it all over
again!*

Giggling, Simone reached into her purse and pulled out
her cell phone. She wanted to do a "drive-by" on Marcus,
but first she had to reschedule her lunch plans. Hoping An-

gela was still at the station, she punched in her number. "Hey, girl," she greeted, pleasantly surprised when her best friend answered on the first ring. "How's it going?"

"Could be better."

"What's wrong? You sound bummed."

Angela paused, then after a long moment, cleared her throat. "*Eye on Chicago* finished last in the ratings again this week."

"Try not to worry. The numbers will pick up."

"I hope so, because I'd rather be a store greeter than return to my old job. I need to be around people, not stuck in a cubicle researching useless facts."

"You've only been on the air for a month. Once viewers find you, they'll watch," Simone said, confident they would. "You're doing a great job, girl, and your segment last night on child beauty pageants was a real eye-opener."

"Thanks, Simone. Talking to you always makes me feel better."

"I am pretty great, aren't I?"

A laugh blasted out of Angela's mouth. "Can we go to that Cajun restaurant downtown for lunch? I'm in the mood for seafood, and they make the best oyster stew in the city."

"About that," Simone began, biting the inside of her cheek. "I can't meet today."

"Why not? I thought you wanted me to help you rewrite your cover letter."

Simone wanted to tell Angela that she had already applied for several caseworker positions online, but didn't. Her best friend got a kick out of sprucing up résumés, and Simone didn't want to disappoint her. "I'm bringing Marcus lunch, and by the time I leave his office it'll be—"

Angela broke in. "When did you start bringing Marcus lunch?"

"When I started reading *A Sista's Guide to Seduction!*"

"Oh, brother, not you, too," she groaned, her tone filled

with angst. "I'm sick of hearing about that stupid pink book. My colleagues have been yakking about it nonstop."

"You should read it, Angela. It's a great book, and who knows, maybe following Dr. RaShondra's rules will lead you straight into the arms of Mr. Right."

"Girl, please, I have a better chance of being struck by lightning!"

The friends laughed.

"Besides, I'm not the one with the problem," Angela insisted. "These Chicago men have some serious issues, and I don't have the time or the energy to deal with their mess."

"That's why you need *A Sista's Guide to Seduction*. You'll learn more about men, gain sexual confidence and view relationships in a whole new light."

"I doubt it."

"I was a skeptical about the book, too," Simone confessed. "But Dr. RaShondra really knows her stuff. I'm only halfway through the book, but I've already noticed subtle changes in Marcus. He still works insane hours, but now he calls to check in and is more affectionate in public."

"Just be careful," Angela warned, her tone stern. "Relationships are about honesty, not game playing and manipulation. No one can tell you how to live your life or how to have a successful relationship, either. The answer is, and always will be, in you."

"Thanks, Oprah Junior."

Angela cracked up. She laughed so loud, Simone had to hold the phone away from her ear.

"Since you're too busy *seducing* your husband to meet me for lunch, I'm going to work on my next segment," she explained, her voice perking up. "I'm doing a piece on professional athletes who've had run-ins with the law, and my producer wants my notes by the end of the day."

"Let's have breakfast tomorrow. You can tell me all about the story then."

"I can't. I have a blind date."

Simone frowned. "In the morning?"

"Yup, breakfast dates are the newest dating craze. I've been on a couple, and although I didn't make any love connections, I had a decent time. The dates are short, and if the dude turns out to be dud, I've only wasted an hour of my time, as opposed to three."

"What do you know about your date?"

"He's an L.A. sports agent in town on business."

Simone heard papers rustle, a door slam and then the chug of a photocopier. "Is he helping you with your segment?"

"You could say that," she replied casually. "I plan to pick his brain about the sports world while we sip our lattes. I like to think of it as killing two birds with one stone."

Simone shook her head. Her best friend was never going to change. Love would always take a backseat to Angela's career, and although she joked about wanting to settle down, Simone knew she wasn't ready. Angela treasured her independence and didn't want a man or love cramping her style.

"Have fun seducing your husband!" Angela quipped, her tone thick with sarcasm. "Don't do anything I wouldn't do."

Girl, I'm going to do things you would never dream of! Simone thought, indulging in a wide, saucy smirk. *By the time I'm finished with Marcus he won't remember his name!*

Chapter 8

The Samson Gym parking lot resembled the Lincoln Park Zoo. As soon as a car exited the complex, five more turned in. Finding a vacant space was an exercise in patience, and at twelve-thirty on a wickedly cold afternoon, Simone was in no mood to wait. Cutting in front of the minivan double-parked in the handicap zone, she squeezed into the empty spot beside the garbage bin and turned off the car. Grabbing the bag of takeout, she took Jayden and Jordan by the hand and led them across the icy parking lot.

"Hey, boys, what's shaking?" said a student trainer as they strode toward the front entrance. "Want to come into the gym and kick around the soccer ball?"

Delight sparked in Jordan's eyes. "Can we, Mom? We promise to be good."

Simone nodded. "Okay. I'll pick you up when I'm finished talking to Daddy."

"Take your time," Jayden said, grabbing the trainer's hand. "See you later, Mommy!"

Off the boys went, laughing and joking with their lanky, blue-eyed friend.

Simone made her way through the cardio room. Fits of grunts and groans and the sound of clanging weights competed with the rock music blaring from the speakers. Aerobic classes were in full swing, and seniors clad in colorful workout gear chatted beside the water fountain.

To limit distractions, Marcus had set up shop in the office at the rear of the gym. It was a small space, with only one window, but he loved the quiet, secluded location. *And I do, too,* she thought. *His office is plain, but it's the perfect location for a secret rendezvous.*

Simone spotted Danica Lewis perusing the snacks in the vending machine. For the life of her, she couldn't figure out why the front-desk clerk would dye her hair black or pierce her tongue, but Danica was Simone's favorite staff member and they got along great. The business major doted on Jayden and Jordan but never let them get out of line. "Hi, Danica," Simone greeted her. "How's school? Maintaining that 4.0 GPA, I hope."

"You know it!"

The women laughed.

"Is Marcus here?" Simone held up the plastic bag. "I brought him lunch."

Danica hustled around the circular desk. "I'll just buzz you in. I'm leaving to run some errands, but I should be back in an hour."

"Great, maybe I'll stick around and join that Boxercise class you've been raving about."

"Sounds good. See you later, Mrs. Young!"

I couldn't have planned this better myself, Simone thought, heading down the long, narrow corridor. *With Danica gone, I don't have to worry about any untimely interruptions.*

Simone found Marcus behind his desk, on the phone, flipping through a manila file folder. His office, though filled with awards, plaques and sports memorabilia, was a stark contrast to his spacious home office. A bookshelf, two chairs and a closet—which housed everything from suits to jeans and runners—were the only furniture in the room.

Simone knocked gently on the door.

Marcus glanced up from his desk. His entire face came alive, brightened with surprise. His smile grabbed her, made her feel light-headed and dizzy. Keeping her hands behind her back, she leaned nonchalantly against the door frame and struck her best come-and-get-me pose.

"Come in," he mouthed, waving her inside. Rolling his eyes wildly, he cupped the mouthpiece and lowered it to his chest. "This fitness equipment rep could talk until the Second Coming of Christ," he joked, shaking his head. "Just hang tight. I'll be off in a minute."

But a minute turned into two, then five, and when Marcus started talking about his upcoming interview with the Chicago Bears, Simone wondered if he remembered she was even there. To remind him, she cleared her throat.

"I'll be in touch." He paused, then said, "Yes. Okay. Bye."

"Finally," she teased, concealing a smile. "I thought you'd never get off the phone."

Marcus dropped the receiver in the cradle. "I didn't know you were stopping by."

"Do I need a reason to come see my gorgeous husband?"

"Of course not, baby. You're always welcome here. Where are Jayden and Jordan?"

"Playing in the kid's gym." Simone stepped inside the office, careful to conceal the plastic bag. "I promised you'd come see them before we leave."

"How has your day been?"

"Okay. I applied for a few part-time jobs, and the boys helped me bake cookies."

Marcus nodded absently, shuffled the papers around on his desk. "How was practice?"

"Don't ask."

"That bad, huh? Let me guess, Jayden cried the whole

time and Jordan shot wildly at the net every five seconds—" Marcus paused and sniffed the air. "Ummm, I smell mozzarella cheese."

"I brought you a steak sandwich, sweet potato fries and a slice of cherry cheesecake." Simone took her hands from behind her back and swung the plastic bag in front of his face. "Tell me where we're going for our romantic weekend getaway and I'll give you all this food."

"That's blackmail!"

"Fess up, or prepare to watch me eat in front of you!"

Chuckling, he pushed back his chair and strode around his desk. "Baby, that's cold. I can't believe you'd stoop so low. What happened to the sweet, loving woman I married?"

"She started watching *Mob Wives* and got a backbone!" Simone tossed her head back and had a good laugh. She was enjoying every minute of their playful banter, and she could tell by the grin on her husband's face that he liked it, too. "Be a good sport, baby. This is all in good fun."

"I never knew you played dirty."

"There's a lot about me you don't know."

Marcus took the bag from her, rested it on his desk and circled his arms around her waist. The scent of her perfume fell over him, stirring his sexual hunger. "I'm glad you stopped by. Seeing you is the best part of my day—"

"Quit trying to sweet-talk me," she sassed, cutting him off midsentence. "I'm not relinquishing the food until you tell me what I need to know, so start talking, Mr. Young."

"Fine, I'll tell you where we're going." Pausing expectantly, he leaned against the desk and crossed his legs at his ankles. "We're going to spend four nights and five days at the world-renowned Chateau LeBlanc in Manchester, Vermont."

Simone blinked hard. She must have misheard Marcus, because it sounded like he said they were going to—she coughed, stumbled over the word—Vermont.

"I know you had your heart set on going to the Dominican

Republic again, but I thought it would be cool to go somewhere nearby, somewhere we've never been before."

The weight of her disappointment was crushing, heavier than hundred-pound weights. Grappling for her words, Simone swallowed the bitter, rancid taste in her mouth. *Who ever heard of trading one wickedly cold place for another?* she wondered, trying to figure out why Marcus would have planned a trip to Vermont. Unless… Her mouth fell open, hit her chest with a thud. *I should have known this trip was too good to be true!* This wasn't a romantic weekend getaway; it was a business trip. Had to be. Why else would he want to go there? "You have a meeting in Manchester, don't you?"

His smile dimmed. "I have a couple appointments lined up the morning we arrive, but after that I'm all yours."

"Can I get that in writing?"

Marcus chuckled. "You don't need to. There's nothing more important to me than spending the weekend with you, and I plan to give you my undivided attention."

Simone brightened at the news. Sure, she was disappointed that they weren't going to an exotic, postcard-perfect island, but a few days alone with her husband sounded like paradise. The truth was, Simone didn't care where they went as long as they were together—and Marcus's cell phone was turned off. "Tell me more about the trip."

"No way," he replied with an adamant shake of his head. "I've already told you too much. Just trust me. We're going to have a blast."

"We are?" Simone frowned. "As far as I know, there isn't a whole lot to do in Manchester besides winter sports, and when it comes to skiing I have two left feet!"

Marcus brushed his nose against her cheek, used his fingertips to draw circles on her back. "I have a ton of activities planned and a romantic evening at the Chateau's spa that you'll never, *ever* forget."

His enthusiasm was contagious, and soon Simone was

wearing a smile as wide as his. "I can't wait to leave," she confessed. "I just hope it isn't freezing cold there."

"Don't worry. I'll be there to warm you up."

"I look forward to it."

His eyes danced over her face, then crawled down her chest.

"All those extra training sessions with that reality star are really paying off," she purred, squeezing his biceps. "You've beefed up a lot these past few months."

His chest inflated with pride. "I love when you stroke my ego."

"And I love when you stroke *me*."

Marcus crushed his lips to her moist, lush mouth. His kiss scorched her, set every nerve ending in her body on fire. Snaking her hands around his neck, she stroked the back of his fine, smooth hair. Simone felt a hint of his tongue and used hers to coax his out of his mouth. Their tongues touched and lapped, played and teased.

Nothing compared to kissing him, to being in his arms. Marcus ravished her with his mouth, kindled her hunger with his lips and lavished words of praise on her. "You're so gorgeous, so ridiculously beautiful," he rasped, brushing his lips across her cheeks. "How in the world did I end up married to a woman as incredible as you?"

Each kiss grew more intense, desperate.

The air became thick, so charged with sexual tension that Simone couldn't breathe. She felt an insane rush of pleasure that pulsed from her nipples to her core. Panting, she clung desperately to him. Marcus lifted her up off her feet, backed her up against the far wall. The room spun, whirled out of control. Her body trembled, hummed, shook like she'd been shocked by a defibrillator. The phone rang, and the loud, incessant noise concealed her moans of passion.

Off went her sweater, his hoodie, their shoes.

Shoving down the straps of her bra, he used his tongue to tickle her cleavage. He cupped her breasts, mashed them together. Marcus blew in her ear, stroked the most sensitive areas of her flesh with his hands and mouth. Grinding himself into her, he rocked and thrust his hips until she was whimpering his name.

Adrenaline kicked in, sent a million tremors shooting through her body. It had never been like this, never, *ever* been this intense. Simone felt alive, energized, like she'd just polished off a whole case of energy drinks.

Caught up in the moment and the pure thrill of doing something so forbidden and reckless, Simone couldn't bring herself to stop. She'd overstayed her welcome, completely disregarded the advice given in chapter five of *A Sista's Guide to Seduction,* but Simone didn't want to leave. Not when Marcus was doing and saying all the right things.

Horny, wet and desperate to feel him inside her, she hooked a leg around his waist. Crazed with desire, a passion so hot it threatened to consume her, she yanked down his boxers and seized him in her hands. His erection grew, doubled in length right before her eyes.

Still stroking his erection, Simone lowered herself to her knees. Gripping his waist, she parted her lips and eagerly sucked him into her mouth. Slowly, as if she had all the time in the world, she swirled her tongue around his shaft, licking, sucking, tasting. Simone didn't know if it was the fact that she was in her husband's office or the prospect of being caught, but pleasuring Marcus made her feel daring, wanton, like a skydiver jumping out of a plane. And the more her husband groaned, the sexier and more powerful she felt.

To control the pace, Marcus cradled her head in his hands. He struggled to remain in control, and when Simone raked her teeth along his shaft, he grunted louder than a tennis player.

Scared he was going to lose his footing, he gripped the side of the closet. Shock and awe filled him, making him feel dazed and confused. Marcus couldn't believe it, couldn't wrap his brain around it. Simone was going down on him, here, in his office, at one o'clock on a Wednesday afternoon? Or was it Thursday?

Marcus grunted, groaned his pleasure. He was losing it, babbling like a six-month-old baby, and if Simone flicked her tongue over his shaft one more time, he was going to bend her over his desk and plunge so deep inside her she'd come on the spot.

"Mr. Young?" Someone knocked on the door, then jiggled the lock. "Hello? It's Jewel."

Marcus felt groggy, like he'd just awoken from an alcohol-induced nap, but he croaked out a coherent response. "Yes, yes, Jewel, what is it?"

"Your lawyer is holding on line one."

"Oh, okay, thanks, but don't put any more calls through."

"No problem, Mr. Young."

Her footsteps faded, then disappeared in the corridor.

"I better get out of here and let you take that call."

Marcus shook his head, but Simone rose to her feet and swiped her clothes up from the floor. In seconds, she was dressed, had her purse in hand and was ready to go.

"Give me a minute, and I'll get rid of Mr. Rosenfeldt."

"It's okay. Take the call. I need to get Jayden and Jordan anyways. Their guitar lesson starts in an hour, and I promised we'd stop for ice cream first."

"Baby, don't leave me like this." His face lined with anguish, he motioned downward and brushed his long, stiff erection against her thighs. "I need you."

Simone gave him a peck on the lips. "I'll tell Jayden and Jordan you'll see them later."

His shoulders sank. "You know this is wrong, right?"

"What?"

"Turning me on, then leaving me hanging."

"It's not my fault your attorney called," she countered, gesturing at the phone.

Grumbling under his breath, he slid on his shirt, zipped up his pants and stuffed his feet back into his shoes. "Fine, leave, but I'm tapping that ass as *soon* as I get home."

"You can't." Simone wore an innocent face. "I'm saving myself."

"For what?"

"Our romantic getaway."

Marcus reached for her, a sparkle in his eyes and a crooked half grin on his lips. "If you're saving yourself for our trip to Manchester, then we're flying out tonight!"

Chapter 9

"Welcome to Manchester, home of the American Fly Fishing Museum," the pilot said, his tone light and jovial. "The local time is 8:45 p.m., and the temperature is—brace yourself, people—a bone-chilling ten degrees and dropping by the second!"

Groans erupted in first class.

"Sit tight, everyone, and we'll have you at the gate in a few minutes…"

Simone sat in her plush reclining seat, sipping sweetened oolong tea. It had a delicious fruity flavor and complemented the chocolate éclair she was nibbling on nicely. Simone still couldn't believe that Marcus had booked them on an evening flight to Manchester, but she was thrilled to be seated comfortably in first class and was enjoying all the perks of flying in style.

The cabin was spacious, the snacks plentiful and the service impeccable. *Marcus said I deserve to be treated in style, and who am I to argue?* Simone envisioned them in their five-star suite, cuddling and kissing and talking well into the night. The thought excited her, caused goose bumps to erupt across her arms. For the rest of the week, she wouldn't have to cook or sweep or remind the boys to clean their rooms. Rest and relaxation were the order of the day, and Simone was so anxious to start their romantic weekend she could hardly sit still.

The local news was on the big screen, but Simone wasn't watching it. Neither was Marcus. He was on his iPad. Had been since they boarded the plane. But Simone didn't mind. Sure, he hadn't spoken to her in hours, but she knew once they reached the Chateau LeBlanc he'd give her his undivided attention. After all, this was *their* weekend to reconnect, their weekend to share and play and love.

"Please ensure you have all your personal items before leaving the aircraft…"

Simone sprang into action. It was her first trip alone with Marcus since the twins had been born, and she was curious to see what wonderful, romantic things her husband had planned. Unbuckling her seat belt, she bent down, shoved her fashion magazines back into her purse and shrugged on her leather jacket. "Baby, we're here." Simone clutched Marcus's leg, squeezed until he glanced up. "The plane just landed."

Taking out his earpiece, he returned the sleek, electronic device to its leather carrying case. "Are you ready to kick off our romantic weekend?"

"You bet I am!" Simone gave an emphatic nod. "I can't believe we're already here."

"I told you this was a good idea."

"I still would have preferred going to the Dominican Republic. We haven't been back there since we got married, and I'd give anything to spend another week at that oceanfront resort."

Marcus winked at her, patted her hands. "Trust me, once you see the Chateau LeBlanc you won't be thinking of anywhere else."

"I hope you're right."

"Of course I am. To guarantee you have a great time, I spent a ton of money—"

"Being romantic isn't about trying to outdo The Donald, Marcus. It's about doing something special and thoughtful for the person you love."

"I wish you would have told me that *before* I dropped a fortune on your engagement ring," he joked, gesturing to the rock on her left hand. "I'm still paying it off!"

Simone laughed, playfully punched his shoulder. "Okay, I admit it, I have a thing for diamonds, but I'd rather spend a weekend alone with you than go shopping anyday."

"Baby, you'll never have to choose...."

Their eyes met, held for a long, tender moment.

"You can have me *and* big, glittery diamonds."

She kissed him then, allowed her tongue to play over his thick, juicy lips.

"I can't wait to get to our cabin." Marcus stroked her neck, placed kisses across her ears and cheeks. "We're going to finish what we started in my office this afternoon."

"We will, after we have dinner and..."

"I'm in charge," he announced, his tone matter-of-fact. "And the first item on our to-do list is to make love. I'm going to make you scream my name."

"Okay, Mr. Man, you're in charge, but we have to eat first. I'm still hungry!"

The seat belt light pinged, and passengers surged to their feet.

Simone gathered her bags and stepped out into the aisle. Smiling graciously at the airline crew standing at the front of the plane, she clasped her husband's hand and followed him into the small, bustling terminal.

Since they hadn't checked any luggage, Marcus hustled Simone through the airport, out of the sliding glass doors and toward the white limousine idling at the snow-packed curb.

"You rented a limo to take us to the hotel?"

"No, I rented a limo for the *whole* weekend."

"But, there's only two of us," she said, her eyes wide with surprise. "And that limo's large enough to fit the entire Jackson family!"

"Never mind that, baby. Just get inside!"

The driver, a silver-haired gentleman with kind eyes, held open the back door.

"Thank you." Simone slid inside before the fierce winter wind blew her away. Stunned by how grand and luxurious the limousine was, she swallowed a squeal of delight. The mirrored ceiling, entertainment unit and the cherrywood bar stocked with beverages and snacks enhanced the stylish decor. The air smelled sweet, and the fragrant watermelon scent caused her mouth to water. "This is amazing! It's like a sleek New York penthouse on wheels!"

"Nothing's too good for you," Marcus said, lifting the remote control off the fridge and pointing it at the entertainment unit. "I'm going to spoil you this weekend, and by the time we return to Chicago you'll be singing my praises."

His cell phone rang, and Simone raised her eyebrows.

Without looking down, Marcus slid his phone out of his pocket and switched it off.

Her smile returned. "That's better."

"Don't worry, baby. There'll be no more interruptions. This weekend is all about you…."

Pleased by his words, Simone sighed inwardly. Pressing herself against the window, she stared at the quaint town nestled against the steep hills. The miles of wide-open fields evoked a sense of calm, of peace. In the distance, Simone saw the jagged profile of snow-topped mountains and a majestic structure that seemed to kiss the sky. "Oh, my goodness," she gushed, overcome by feelings of awe and wonder. "That must be the Chateau. It's as tall as the heavens!"

Marcus opened a bottle of rosé cognac, filled two wine flutes and gave one to her. Mischief shone in his eyes, and the hand resting on her thigh was climbing fast. "Let's make a toast," he proposed, raising his glass in the air. "To a weekend filled with fun, excitement and lots of great sex."

"I'll drink to that." And she did, downing the peach-flavored drink in two quick gulps.

Marcus slid the universal remote control out of the wall pocket. "It's too quiet in here. We need some music. Any requests?"

"Anything but rap. I know you have a guy crush on Lil' Wayne, but not tonight, okay?"

Chuckling, he used the remote to raise the glass divider and lower the overhead lights. Turning on the stereo, he selected a seventies album and settled beside Simone.

R & B music flowed out of invisible speakers, creating a sensual, relaxed mood.

"I love this song." Singing along with Sam Cooke, the legendary soul singer with the remarkable voice, Simone found herself reflecting on the poignant lyrics of his smash hit "A Change Is Gonna Come."

This is more than just a weekend getaway, she decided, gazing up at her husband, love and longing filling her heart. *This is our chance for a fresh start.* "Every time I hear this song, I think about the night we met. It was the first song we ever danced to."

"I know. I remember."

Marcus gave her a long, lusty look, one Simone saw as clearly as the moon in the sky.

"That's why I put it on. So we could reminisce about all the good times."

Cupping her shoulders, he turned her toward the window and nuzzled his chin playfully against her neck. Kneading her muscles with his palms, he used his long, slender fingers to stroke and caress her. His hands were firm, his touch light, the massage so soothing she felt like curling up in his arms and settling in for the night.

His mouth mapped a trail from her shoulder blade to her ear and back again. Over and over. His lips scorched her, filled her with such hunger and passion, she couldn't think. Only feel. Want. Desire. Simone's head fell back, and when Marcus showered kisses down the front of her neck, a purr slipped from her mouth.

Her brain turned to mush.

Her vision blurred.

Her clit pulsed and throbbed and tingled.

Simone felt his tongue part her lips, seeking, imposing. She couldn't catch her breath, couldn't stop her heartbeat from roaring in her ears. His kiss aroused her, instantly put her in the mood for loving. Not that Simone planned on having sex in the limo. She wasn't crazy. Or an exhibitionist. Having a quickie with the silver-haired driver only inches away was something inebriated couples did, and Simone was as sober as a baby. But once they reached the Chateau LeBlanc and checked into their cabin, it was on like Donkey Kong!

Marcus slipped a hand underneath her sweater, caressed her smooth, warm flesh. "I love the way you feel, the way you smell, how delicious you taste…."

Simone tossed a look over her shoulder. A grin curled his lips and lit his eyes.

He fiddled with the front clasp on her bra until her breasts popped out, then flicked his thumb over her nipples. Her skin prickled from the heat of his touch, grew wet and clammy. Simone shook her head, covered his hands with her own. Her body was throbbing, every single nerve, but she was determined to be the voice of reason. "Baby, what are you doing?" she asked, knowing full well what was on her husband's mind.

"Just go with the flow."

"I want you, too, Marcus, but this isn't the time *or* the place."

"I've always dreamed of having sex in a limo," he confessed, stroking her shoulders.

"What if the driver's secretly watching us? Angela did a story last month on hidden cameras in public places, and you wouldn't believe some of the things people did when they thought no one was looking."

"I seriously doubt we're the first couple to ever have sex in his limo."

Frowning, Simone leaned forward and carefully inspected the leather upholstery. "Yuck, that's gross. Now, I *definitely* don't want to make love in here."

"But I've been wanting you all day."

"You have?"

"Ever since you left my office. I wanted to do you in the airplane bathroom, but I knew you'd never go for it." He ran his index finger down her arm. "Fantasies are meant to be fulfilled, and when the mood strikes you should go for it...."

Simone hid a smile. Marcus sounded like Dr. RaShondra, and she couldn't help wondering if he'd snuck a peek at chapter nine, the short, titillating section entitled "Anytime, Anyplace." According to Dr. RaShondra, men craved spontaneity and loved unpredictable women. Don't do anything crazy like giving him oral action in your neighborhood park, she'd cautioned, but don't routinely reject him, either. A Seductress was always in the mood, always ready and willing to please her man. She was down for whatever, wherever. She indulged in his fantasies, talked dirty in bed and sent him salacious text messages throughout the day. To keep the fires blazing, a Seductress talked sexy, walked sexy and dressed sexy at all times....

"We'll be quick..." His lips tickled her neck, and his fingers caressed her stomach.

"What if the driver overhears us and calls the police?" she said, still thinking about Angela's riveting, eye-opening segment. "We could get arrested for indecent exposure, or worse, find ourselves the victim of some creepy online voyeur."

Marcus turned off the lights and cranked up the volume on the stereo. Now the limo was bathed in a dazzling array of colors and the music was deafening.

"I still have a bad feeling about this—"

The limo pitched violently to the right, sending Simone flying into Marcus's arms. Alarmed, her heart thundering in her chest, she glanced out the window. The roads were slick, caked with so much ice that when the limo started up a steep, winding road, Simone feared it was going to slide back down.

"Sorry about that, Mr. and Mrs. Young. I was trying to avoid hitting a deer," a male voice said through the intercom. "I assure you the rest of your ride will be smooth and comfortable."

Simone released the breath she was holding.

His grasp on her waist tightened, making her feel safe and snug in his arms. As she parted her lips to speak, to tell him how excited she was about their romantic weekend getaway, his mouth settled over hers. The taste of his lips and the gentle stroke of his caress accelerated her need. Marcus dipped his tongue farther into her mouth, tasting, drinking, sucking.

The kiss was filled with such passion, such desire, Simone's fears of getting caught in the act evaporated in thin air. A Seductress was always primed and raring to go, and even though she was breaking a commandment or two, making love in the backseat of a sleek, white limo was the ultimate rush. The more Marcus kissed her, moving his tongue freely around her mouth and nibbling on her lips like they were a piece of tropical fruit, the harder it was for Simone to stay in control. It was hard—damn hard to resist Marcus. He felt good, smelled amazing and made her so hot with desire she was quivering all over.

Her conscience attacked her, insisted that what she was doing was wrong. And it was. She was a mother, a respected member of her community, a volunteer. Having sex in a limo—even a pimped-out one with chrome rims and tinted windows—was so...so... Simone couldn't finish her thought. Not when Marcus was palming her breasts and grinding his erection against her thigh.

Straddling his lap, Simone gripped his shoulders and held on tight. The air was thick, filled with their passion, and it made her feel intoxicated. Simone lobbed her arms around his neck and rocked against his erection. Never had she felt so sexy, so desirable. Her desire was feverish, out of control. "Do. Me. Now."

"I'd love nothing more," he said, unbuckling his jeans. "Take off that sweater."

Clothes sailed in the air, fell to the floor like the snowflakes falling from the sky.

Kissing him senselessly, she dragged her nails up and down and over his strong arms. Marcus murmured in her ear, said things that would make anyone blush. The sensual texture of his voice, that silky smooth tone oozing with passion, made her pulse quicken. His mouth was everywhere. On her neck, her shoulders, hungrily lapping between her breasts. He touched her in the right way, in the right places, just the way she liked, giving her exactly what her body needed.

To excite him, she whipped her head around like a stripper dangling from a pole. Marcus ate it up. Cheering her on, he watched with growing interest as she gyrated her hips to the beat of the music. "God, I love you," he breathed. He held her tight then, so close Simone could feel his heart beating through his striped crewneck sweater.

Clutching the back of his head, she purred into his ear, then licked and seized the lobe between her teeth. A siren whirled in the distance, grew so loud it drowned out the music. Simone squinted, stared out into the darkness. Steam fogged up the back windows, making it impossible to see, but the blinding glare of headlights flooded the limo. Had the driver heard their moans and called the police? Where the boys in blue en route to arrest them?

"You feel so good, baby. I could never, ever get enough of you." Marcus massaged her sweet spot through her panties, caressed and tickled and massaged it until she was squirming beneath him, trying to get away. His hands rode her clit, probing and pleasing. In and out, his fingers stroked. Simone raised her shoulders, arched her back like a prizewinning equestrienne mounting a horse. Marcus stirred his finger inside her, gave her everything she needed and more. The song playing on the stereo had a slow, languid beat, but his strokes were quick, deep.

"I'm coming!"

Simone couldn't believe it. She'd never come this fast before, never felt like crying and screaming at the same time. Swathing her arms around his neck, she rotated her hips, rocked hard against his long, thick erection. Flushed, as out of breath as a champion swimmer, she gulped furiously for air. Tilting her head back, she closed her eyes and soaked in the pleasing sounds of their mingled moans and groans.

"We will be arriving at the Chateau LeBlanc in the next five minutes." The driver's deep voice silenced the music and filled the backseat of the limo. "I've notified the concierge of your arrival, and he will be waiting at the front entrance to meet us."

Grinning, Marcus snatched his clothes up off the floor and slid on his shirt. "We better hurry up and get dressed. We're almost there."

"You're not backing out on me, are you?"

"Don't worry. As soon as we get to our cabin I'm taking you straight to the bedroom."

Simone shook her head. No way was she stopping. Not now. Not when she was on the verge of a second, more explosive orgasm. "I can't wait," she breathed, roughly tweaking his nipples with her thumbs. "I need you now, baby. *Right now*."

Marcus's jaw hit the floor. *What has gotten into her?* They'd always had a great sex life, and on occasion Simone even initiated lovemaking, but she'd never been this aggressive, this spontaneous. Ten minutes ago she was against having sex in the limo, and now she was roughing him up. Marcus loved it, but he had to put a stop to it. As exciting as this was, he didn't want to tarnish his reputation. This was the type of story that ended up on the internet, and he didn't want to be the focus of some cheap gossip blog. "We have the whole weekend to make love, and…"

Smiling coyly, she pressed a finger to her lips and shook her head. "Enough talking."

Simone eased forward, slid closer and closer until his erection was buried deep inside her. Gathering steam, she furiously rotated her hips like she was spinning a hula hoop. Licking from his neck to his ear, she pushed Marcus to the brink. He grunted, groaned. And when Simone drew his nipple into her mouth, sucking on it as if it was a chocolate-flavored lollipop, he shot over the edge. He thrust himself inside her, hard and fast.

Simone felt weightless, lighter than air. Pleasure rushed down her back, tickled her all over. The muscles between her legs contracted. Simone pressed her hands against the wall and ordered her quivering limbs to quit shaking. To deepen the penetration, she clamped her thighs around his waist and held on for dear life. Pressed together, hands and legs entwined, they moved together as one, giving, loving, pleasing.

Marcus ran his hands through her hair, grabbed a handful. Having her hair pulled made Simone climax, and when he hiked her legs in the air and increased his thrust, a hard, fast orgasm barreled through him. It was debilitating, as powerful as any earthquake, and Marcus couldn't move if his life depended on it. That's why when the limo stopped and he heard a soft rap on the passenger side window, he called out, "Come back in an hour!"

Chapter 10

I'm going to love it here, Simone decided, waiting patiently while Marcus checked them into the Chateau LeBlanc. Loosening the knot on her knit scarf, she openly admired the hotel's chic, elegant main floor. Talk about grand! A fortune had been spent decorating the lobby with antique furniture, low-hanging lights and plush area rugs, and the lounge looked so inviting Simone wanted to stretch out on the couch and take a snooze.

"Good evening, Mr. and Mrs. Young."

Simone turned just in time to see a slight, clean-cut gentleman pick up their bags.

"Hello, my name is Jules, and I'll be your butler for the duration of your stay." He reached out and shook their hands. "If you follow me, I'd be happy to escort you to your cabin."

They walked through the lobby and were greeted by hotel staff every step of the way. Next to the café was a high-end boutique, and as they passed the front window, Simone decided to return in the morning for a quick look around. Shopping would keep her occupied while Marcus was at his meeting, and by the time he returned she'd be dressed and ready for dinner.

Outside, stars crowded the moon and the wind whipped through the trees surrounding the opulent Chateau. "It's so beautiful up here, so quiet." Inhaling the pine air, Simone marveled at how lush and expansive the hotel grounds were. Nestled on seven acres of land blessed with sweeping mountain views, the Chateau LeBlanc was comprised of private cabins and cottages just steps away from the main building. The groomed trails were wide and steep and stretched to unbelievable distances, beyond what her eyes could see.

"Baby, look," Marcus said, pointing to the lake. "We should rent some skates tomorrow and go for a spin around the rink."

"You go. I'll watch."

"Come on, it'll be fun."

"No, it won't," she argued, shaking her head adamantly. "I'll probably break my arm, and at my age there's nothing cute about wearing a plaster cast!"

The couple laughed.

"Here we are. Cabin Equinox." Jules strode briskly toward the cedar wood cabin and unlocked the door. Stepping aside, he flicked on the lights. "I trust that you'll feel at home here and find everything to your liking."

Marcus whistled. "This place is tight."

You can say that again! An elaborate flower arrangement sat on the kitchen table, dark wood furniture beautified the main floor and the stone fireplace offered warmth and light. With windows on each side of the suite, the forest was visible from anywhere in the room.

"This is our most popular cabin," Jules explained, resting their bags on the living room floor. "Over the years we've had dignitaries, TV personalities and even a young, charismatic presidential candidate stay here with us."

"TV personalities? A presidential candidate? Really?" Simone asked, stunned by the unexpected revelation. "Anyone we know?"

"We pride ourselves on being discreet here at the Château LeBlanc." Jules leaned in and glanced around as if he was afraid someone might overhear him. "But I will say this, she's a global icon with a heart of gold, and he was your state senator for seven years."

Simone gasped. "No way!"

Jules nodded, wearing a smile that displayed every perfectly white tooth.

Wait until I tell Angela and the girls! Simone thought, drunk with excitement. She could see their wide eyes, gaping mouths and stunned expressions now. Simone wanted to know what movies Oprah ordered on pay-per-view and what the Obamas ate for breakfast, but before she could grill their affable butler, Marcus dismissed him.

"Thanks for escorting us to our cabin, Jules. Good night."

"Would you like me to fix you a snack while you unwind upstairs in the master wing?" he asked, taking off his cap and tucking it under his arm. "I went to culinary school in the South of France, and I don't mean to brag, but David Beckham told me my quiche is to die for."

Marcus shook his head. "We're good."

"Very well. If you need anything, just buzz the front desk and I'll be right over." A curt nod and he was gone.

"I can't believe the Obamas stayed here!" Simone gushed, clearly awestruck.

"That's nothing," Marcus said with a dismissive shrug of his shoulders. "I have a lot more in store for you, and a surprise on Sunday night that's sure to knock you off your feet!"

Elated, Simone threw her arms around his neck and kissed him so hard he dropped into the leather chair. She stroked his face, sprayed kisses on his forehead, cheeks and along his jaw.

"Wow, if I knew you'd be *this* excited, I would've brought you here a long time ago!"

Happiness shone in her eyes and filled her voice. "Thanks for planning this weekend for us, Marcus. It means a lot to me."

"I'll do anything for you, Simone. You know that."

Simone caressed his chest with the palms of her hands. She pressed her body against his, made sure he felt her erect nipples and the softness of her warm flesh.

"Save some of that passion for later," he advised, winking at her. "We're going to experiment tonight in the bedroom and you're going to need your strength…."

Lust blazed in his eyes and seeped into his smooth, silky tone.

Simone could only image what Marcus had in store for her. Having a quickie in the limousine was exhilarating, and Simone was still reeling from her multiple orgasms. They had the entire weekend to themselves, and the sly grin on Marcus's face suggested they were probably going to spend most of it making love. "I wish we could stay here for a month."

"You do?"

"You don't?"

"I enjoy getting away from time to time, but I'd miss going into the office." A smile fell across his lips. "And we have two great kids at home who need us."

"I know, it's just…" Simone hesitated, wavered between sharing her thoughts and keeping them to herself. Since Marcus was in a great mood, and they were having a nice time, she decided to share her heart. "Sometimes things are so good between us. We talk and laugh and you make me feel like I'm the most important person in your life, and other times—"

"I hate when you talk like that," he interrupted, cutting in.

"Talk like what?"

"You make it sound like our marriage is in trouble and it's not. Every relationship goes through ups and downs, and we're no different than any other couple."

"I know, but—"

"But what?" His body stiffened, became ice-cold.

"I wish you had more of a traditional schedule, like other fathers, that's all. Sometimes the kids and I don't see you for days, and it's tough doing everything by myself."

"Simone, you're so busy comparing our marriage to everyone else's you don't see how good we have it."

"That's not it."

"Then what is it?" he demanded, sliding her legs off his waist and standing up. "Because I'm sick of hearing what a crappy husband and father I am."

Simone surged to her feet. "Don't put words into my mouth, Marcus. I never once said that you were a bad father."

"You didn't have to. I can read between the lines."

"When have I ever said that—"

He waved off her question with a flick of his hand. "Forget it. I didn't come all this way to argue, and that's exactly where this conversation is headed."

"At least we agree on one thing," Simone mumbled, stunned by the sudden change of events. One minute they were cuddled up, kissing and playing like a couple of teenagers, and the next they were at each other's throats. *What's up with that?* she thought, noting Marcus's narrowed gaze and rigid posture. *Can't I share my feelings without him blowing up at me?*

To regroup, she took a deep breath. As Simone exhaled, a salacious image flashed in her mind's eye. A grin came. Inside the limousine, they'd made love so passionately, so urgently, she was eager for round two. This was their weekend to reconnect, and Simone didn't want to waste a second of it arguing. They did enough of that at home.

Determined to get their evening back on track, she decided a dip in the hot tub was just what the doctor ordered, but as she opened her mouth to suggest it, Marcus's cell phone buzzed.

"I'm going to go into the office," he said casually. "I need to make some calls."

Simone nodded and smiled to hide her disappointment. "Oh, okay, I guess I'll go unpack then."

"I'll be back in a few."

"Meet me in the bedroom."

Surprise flashed across Marcus's face. The corners of his

lips were twitching, and his gaze was smoldering with lust. "Give me ten minutes."

"I'll be waiting...."

Bags in hand, Simone climbed the stairs to the second floor. The cottage had all the comforts of home, and when she saw the toy-filled bonus room next to the den, her thoughts turned to Jayden and Jordan. A smile touched her mouth when she remembered the scene at the airport. Jayden sniffling, clutching her legs, Jordan jumping on and off the luggage carts, shrieking with delight. Simone missed her boys, and although she knew they weren't problem kids, she could only imagine what trouble they were giving Grandma Gladys at home.

Glancing at her watch, she decided it wasn't too late to call, and she dialed her home number. When no one answered, she tried her mother-in-law's cell phone. "Hello?"

Simone heard a rustling sound, giggling, then Jayden's high-pitched voice on the line.

"Hi, Mommy!"

"Hey, baby," she greeted, a grin overwhelming her lips. "How are you doing?"

"Great! Mommy, can I have a mohsikel?"

"A what?"

"A mohsikel," he repeated, nice and loud.

"What's that?"

"A bike that people ride on the street."

Simone laughed. "Oh, baby, you mean a mo-tor-cy-cle."

"That's what I said, Mommy. So, can I get one? Please?"

Simone frowned, stared down at the receiver. It sounded like Jayden, but he would never make such an outlandish request. Now Jordan was another story.

"Uncle Derek took me for a ride on his shiny new motorcycle, and it was so much fun!"

Simone's heart stopped dead in her chest.

"He bought me ice cream, too, Mommy. And it had sprinkles and chocolate syrup."

He giggled and said something Simone didn't understand.

"Jayden, honey, put Grandma on the phone."

"Okay, Mommy. Bye!"

A second later, Gladys came on the line, chatting a mile a minute.

"How was your flight? Everything okay? Have you guys checked into your hotel yet?"

"Did Jayden go for a ride on Derek's motorcycle?" Simone asked, hoping her son's tale was a figment of his overactive imagination.

"Well, hello to you, too."

Simone took a moment, waited until she was calm before she spoke again. "Gladys, we really appreciate you watching Jayden and Jordan on such short notice, but we expect you—"

"But nothing! Don't talk to me like I'm one of the boys. I'm twice your age, missy."

Shocked by the sharpness of her mother-in-law's tone, Simone slumped against the dresser, wide-eyed and tongue-tied. She couldn't believe this was happening. Again. Couldn't believe that Gladys was attacking her. Again.

Simone swallowed her retort. Marcus had promised to talk to his mom, had sworn up and down that Gladys would stick to the schedule this time, but he obviously hadn't said a word to her. And that pissed Simone off.

"Jayden wanted to go for a spin on his uncle's bike, and I didn't see a problem with it."

Of course you didn't, Simone thought, gritting her teeth. *You think you're perfect!*

"I don't want the boys eating junk food all day long or riding on Derek's bike, either." Simone spoke calmly, but inside she was boiling mad. Closing her eyes, she took a deep breath and prayed for restraint. Because right now, she wanted to reach through the phone and shake Gladys until her wig fell off.

"Why are you being so uptight? The boys are having a great time, so relax."

"Gladys, there's a food chart on the fridge beside the boys' schedule, so if you're unsure about something, just double-check."

"We're not at the house, so I'll just have to wing it this weekend."

Simone frowned. "Where are you?"

"At my place, of course."

"Why?"

"Because the boys want to spend the night," she explained hotly. "They're having so much fun playing with the neighborhood kids they wouldn't even come inside for dinner."

To stop from voicing the words running through her mind, Simone slid her tongue along the front of her teeth. Her mother-in-law was crazy. Officially off her rocker. Why else would she take Jayden and Jordan to her house halfway across town and let them do whatever they wanted? Simone didn't want her sons anywhere near Gladys's on-again, off-again boyfriend, and if she thought there was a red-eye flight to Chicago, she'd be on the first thing smokin' out of Manchester. "I'll give you a call tomorrow," Simone said through clenched teeth. "What time will you be back at the house?"

"I wasn't planning on going back."

"But Jordan has a dentist appointment at eleven-thirty."

"I'll try to be there on time, but I promised the boys I'd take them to see a movie at Sherbrooke Mall, and I don't want to disappoint them."

"Tell my mom I said hi."

At the sound of her husband's voice, Simone spun around. Marcus must have seen the smoke coming out of her ears, because the broad smile sitting on his lips slid off his face. He wore a troubled expression, one that wrinkled his forehead and eyebrows. "What's the matter? Are the boys okay?" he asked, striding toward her.

"Is that Marcus?" Gladys chirped. "Put him on. I need to talk to him."

That makes two of us!

Simone pointed the receiver at him. "Set your mother straight, Marcus, or I will."

Pacing the length of the room didn't help calm Simone down, but it was either walk off her frustration or wrestle the phone away from Marcus and tell Gladys off. She watched Marcus stretch out on the bed and close his eyes. He looked serene, at ease, like he was luxuriating on a tropical beach.

Simone waited for Marcus to scold his mom for being irresponsible, but the rebuke never came. And when he hung up the phone seconds later, he was actually grinning. *How come he's not upset?* His brother had put Jayden in harm's way, and Simone refused to turn a blind eye, refused to brush this under the rug. No way. No how. Prepared to war, she arched her shoulders and folded her arms. "Did Gladys tell you that Jayden went for a ride on Derek's motorcycle?"

"Yeah, Mom said she's never seen him so excited!"

Simone blinked, shook her head. "I can't believe this…."

"I know, huh? The kid hates bugs, but he loves motorcycles! Go figure!" Marcus chuckled. "I told mom to make sure Jayden wears a helmet the next time—"

"That's it? That's all you said?"

"What else is there to say?"

"How about, 'He's not allowed on that bike again!'" she snapped, throwing her hands up in the air. "Jayden's five, not fifteen. He has no business being on Derek's motorcycle."

"D.'s been riding bikes since he was a kid. He's the safest driver I know."

"Yeah, when he's not stoned out of his mind…."

"He doesn't smoke anymore."

"Sure he doesn't, that's why he can't keep a job longer than a week."

"D.'s been working full-time since March, but you'd know that if you talked to him when he called instead of passing the phone off to me."

Simone swallowed a retort, one that was sure to pour more gasoline on the fire. The truth was, she had no interest in talking to her brother-in-law or anyone else in her husband's family. Being raised in the inner city herself, Simone knew how difficult it was growing up in government housing neighborhoods, but she didn't condone violence of any kind and Marcus's older brother enjoyed living on the wrong side of the law. If it were up to her, she would see Derrek only during the holidays. But she had children who adored their uncle, so for the sake of her sons she put up with her husband's wayward sibling.

"I don't understand why you're so upset. It was a ten-second ride—"

"Without a helmet, on an icy street, after dark," she added, spitting out the words.

Marcus opened his mouth, then quickly closed it.

"Last month, I forgot to buckle Jordan into his seat belt, and you reamed me out, but it's okay for your brother to take Jayden for a spin around the block on his motorcycle? Tell me how what I did was wrong, but what Derek did is right?"

Silence descended, settled over the master suite like thick, lung-scorching smoke.

"This was a bad idea. We never should have come here."

More silence.

"I'm sorry, baby, you're right." Marcus held out his hands. An apologetic expression covered his face, and his voice was filled with remorse. "Anything could have happened...."

His declaration stunned Simone, left her speechless.

"Jayden could have fallen or gotten seriously hurt."

Simone had been thinking the same thing, but she couldn't bring herself to actually speak the words. Not about her baby. Being a social worker, she'd seen firsthand how quickly life changed, how accidents involving minors devastated lives. That's why she was angry.

"I'll call Mom back later."

Simone wanted Marcus to call Gladys now, but she decided not to push it. They were finally on the same page, and that was enough for her. She wanted Marcus to spend more time with her and the boys, and she was willing to do anything to improve their marriage. Simone knew how to get her husband's attention, and she hoped once she met his needs in the bedroom he'd be more receptive to what she had to say. Isn't that what the little pink book guaranteed?

Marcus reached for her, pulled her into the safety of his strong, powerful arms. For a long moment, they stood there, in silence, enjoying the feel of being so intimate, so close. The scent of his cologne fell over her, and the light, refreshing fragrance evoked thoughts of making sweet love. Marcus ran his fingers through her hair, twirled and coiled the ends.

"Want me to order in some room service?" he asked, assuming a tone as crisp and formal as their personal butler. "I hear the quiche is to die for."

Simone giggled. "No, thanks. I'm good."

"But I thought you were hungry?"

"I am," she conceded, touching a hand to his chest. "But not for food...."

Marcus raised an eyebrow. "Do tell."

"I've always fantasized about making love on a bearskin rug."

"Is that right?"

"Are you game?"

"Hell, yeah, I'm game!" Scooping her up in his arms, he set off across the room toward the fireplace. "Come on, baby. Let's kick off our romantic weekend right!"

Chapter 11

"Miss Universe ain't got nothin' on me!" Simone shrieked, striking a fierce pose in front of the full-length bathroom mirror. "I'm not stick-thin with fake boobs, but I'm one bad mama jama!"

Giggling, she hiked her foot up on the bathtub and zipped up her leather boots. It was Saturday night, and Simone was ready for a night out on the town. To complete her va-va-va-voom look, she gathered her hair in her hands and pulled it up into a high, sleek ponytail. Encrusted in diamonds, the silver clip gave her instant glamour and made her appear youthful and sophisticated. A few gold accessories, a spritz of perfume and Simone was done. Ready for her six-o'clock dinner date with her gorgeous husband. Simone couldn't wait to tell Marcus about the job offer she'd received that morning from the director of Friendship House. Anxious to see him, she did one final twirl in the mirror and turned off the lights.

Tucking her metallic clutch purse under her arm, she strode into the living room with her shoulders squared and her head held high. Just like a supermodel gliding down a Paris runway. At the front window, Simone pulled back the silk drapes and stared outside. No sign of Marcus, but plenty of activity going on around the Chateau LeBlanc. Families skated on the rink, guests socialized in front of the lodge and starry-eyed couples strolled along the trails.

Simone peered down the road, hoping to catch a glimpse of the stretch limo. She couldn't wait to see the look on Marcus's face when he saw her outfit. Thanks to the boutique owner, Simone felt like a million bucks. Marcus was always imploring her to show off her legs, so she'd selected a ruffled minidress that kissed her thighs. The clingy burgundy number gave her a slim silhouette and made her waist appear smaller, which was a definite plus.

Glancing at the wall clock, Simone realized she was ready fifteen minutes early. She thought of calling Jayden and Jordan, but remembered they were at the movies with Gladys.

On the coffee table, she spotted *A Sista's Guide to Seduction* and picked it up. All day, she'd been running around, getting pricked and plucked and waxed, and she relished having a few quiet minutes to herself. Simone had only one more chapter left to read of the titillating self-help book, and she had a feeling the good doctor had saved the best for last.

Opening the little pink book, Simone settled into the armchair in front of the fireplace and crossed her legs. Outside, snow was falling in sheets. The wind was howling, beating the tree branches against the windows, but the cabin was cozy, filled with such warmth and tranquility, it was easy to ignore Mother Nature's fury. Simone read the title of the epilogue, and frowned. *If it's broke, fix it? Dr. RaShondra sure has a way with words,* she thought, laughing to herself.

I've given you dozens of tips and ideas on how to seduce the man of your dreams, and if you follow my advice, he'll be worshipping the ground you walk on! I've done my part, ladies. Now the rest is up to you. I leave you with one last piece of advice. Do not, I repeat, do not be anyone's doormat. If he doesn't want you, let him go... I think the R & B singer Mya said it best: "It's all about me, me, me, me, me, forget about you, you, you, you, you." Women have the tendency to want to be everything to everybody. It's not enough for us to be a girlfriend, a wife, a lover. No, we want to be a therapist, a doctor, a pastor, a lawyer. We think we can run his life better than he can. It's not enough for us to give advice and let it be. No, we feel compelled to fix whatever's wrong. Girl, you're not a Ms. Fix-It. If he doesn't want you, let his rusty butt go! And work hard at being the best woman, sister, daughter, friend that you can be. Spend time enlightening your mind, feeding your soul, developing your inner and outer beauty and enriching the lives of others. A Seductress does not wait around for him to call and refuses to be disrespected. She has her own life to live and no time to waste chasing after a man who doesn't want her. Okay?

The telephone rang. *I hope Marcus isn't calling to cancel,* Simone thought, shooting across the living room floor. Worried she was going to miss the call, she snatched the receiver off the cradle and panted a breathless "Hello?"

"Hey, baby. What's shaking?"

"Nothing much. Just waiting for you to get back. Are you, um, on your way?"

"I'll be there soon. Give or take five minutes."

At the sound of his voice, a smile warmed her lips. They'd been married so long, she could tell what kind of mood Marcus was in by his tone, and it was obvious her husband was very excited about something. "I guess I don't have to ask how your meeting went…."

"They loved my idea of filming a competition-type reality show at Samson's and promised to get back to me by the end of the month," he explained. "The studio head said they need time to work out the logistics, but that was just a front. I've got it in the bag!"

"That's wonderful! Now, we have two things to celebrate tonight."

"Baby, what's your good news?"

"Remember that woman's clinic I was telling you about?" A pause, then "No."

"The one that opened last month on the South Side?"

Her question was met with silence.

"Anyways, they HR director at Friendship House wants me to come in—"

"For what?" he questioned, his tone turning serious.

"They're looking for a part-time case manager."

"So, why are they calling you?"

"Because I sent in my résumé, Einstein!" Simone laughed, shook her head. Marcus knew every pro football player by name, all their stats and personal history, but he couldn't remember the conversation they'd had a week earlier. Go figure. "I applied for fun, just to test the waters, so I was stunned when the HR director called me and practically offered me the job. We talked for almost an hour, and at the end of our conversation, Mrs. Alvarez invited me to come in next week to check out the center. Isn't that great?"

"And what will Jayden and Jordan be doing while you're off working?"

Simone stared down at the receiver. She heard the edge in her husband's tone, the shift from playful banter to stone-cold seriousness. "I'll work while the boys are at school. The position is only twenty hours a week, and they're open to me working evenings and weekends."

"I see...." Marcus paused, cleared his throat. "Are you dressed and ready to go?"

"I sure am."

"Cool. Meet me out front in five minutes."

"I'm on my way."

Snatching her purse off the chair, she whipped her shawl

around her shoulders and hurried through the cabin and out the front door. Walking along the icy path in stiletto boots was nerve-racking and if the blue-eyed concierge hadn't rushed to her aid, she would have slid to the ground in a heap of Prada couture. "Thank you so much—" Simone smiled and paused to read his name tag "—Luca."

"It's my pleasure. Can't have a beautiful guest like you getting hurt on my watch."

Upon reaching the lobby, Simone slipped a twenty-dollar bill out of her purse and stuffed it into his front pocket. "You're a lifesaver. I couldn't have made it here without you."

"It was no trouble at all." His eyes dipped to her cleavage, settled there for a long beat. "Have a good night."

"I will, and you enjoy the rest of your evening, as well."

The concierge didn't move. He remained in place, his gaze sliding down her hips and curves. "We're not supposed to fraternize with guests," he began, ruffling his mop of thick, black hair, "but I've been kicking myself all day for not approaching you when I spotted you outside the spa earlier."

Glancing around, he leaned forward and dropped his voice to a throaty whisper. "You're an incredibly gorgeous woman, and if you're not busy tomorrow I'd love to take you for coffee."

Simone's felt her eyes bulge, pop square out of her head. Imagine that! This young, cute Zac Efron look-alike was hitting on her! Concealing a smile, she held up her left hand and pointed to her diamond wedding ring. "I'm married—"

"Happily?"

Simone wore a straight face, but inside she was cracking up. The hotel concierge had some serious game, and his infectious smile was a killer. "My husband should be here any minute now," she explained, glancing at the revolving doors. "He's taking me out for a dinner."

"How nice." His tone was as stiff as his upper lip. "Do you have any sisters or friends as beautiful as you are?"

Simone told Luca that he should catch the first flight to

L.A. because he could have a bright future in Tinseltown. More laughter came, and soon they were chatting about their favorite movies and trading jokes like longtime friends.

Seated at the hotel bar drinking a scotch on the rocks, Marcus watched the exchange between his wife and the obviously smitten concierge with growing interest. Amused, he looked on as the kid handed Simone his business card. This happened all the time. He couldn't leave his wife alone for ten seconds without someone approaching her.

Marcus shook his head and shrugged. He didn't mind, though. Simone was stunning, the single most beautiful woman in the room, and he was proud that she carried his last name. And tonight she was working the hell out of that burgundy minidress. Fashionably dressed in a tight, hot number that showed off every mouthwatering curve, her long ponytail swishing against her back, his wife looked sexier than ever before.

His heart beat in double time. Marcus couldn't wait to get her out of that dress and into bed. But first, he had to romance her. Charm her. Show her that she was still the woman of his dreams. Thinking out of the box had never been his specialty, but he'd promised his wife a memorable evening and he planned to deliver. And if he was lucky, she'd forget all about getting a part-time job. For one, they didn't need the money, and he hated the thought of her running herself ragged when she should be at home with him and the boys. Truth be told, he hated the idea of Simone returning to work. The only thing he wanted her to work on was getting pregnant. He wanted more children—lots more—and the sooner she had a little bun in the oven, the better.

Marcus thought about last night. After making love, they'd headed over to the hotel lounge to grab a bite to eat. They dined on prime rib, shared a fifty-year-old bottle of wine, then took a short walk through the grounds. Strolling along one of the many trails, the light from the moon illuminating the path, they'd reminisced about their first date. Then, before turning back, they'd stopped in a thicket of pine trees and kissed so deeply, so intensely, he'd almost lost his footing. Thinking about it now, and seeing Simone in *that* dress, made Marcus want to ravish her.

Time to go get my wife, he decided, downing the rest of his drink. Marcus stood, dropped a tip on the counter and strode out of the bar. Wearing a proud smile, he greeted the hotel concierge with a nod of his head, slipped an arm around Simone and led her through the lobby. "Are you trying to get me killed?" he teased, dropping a kiss on her cheek.

"Is that your way of telling me I look great?"

"You look better than great, that's why that young pup was champing at the bit!"

Simone wore an innocent face. "What? He was just making small talk."

"Sure, he was. Five more minutes of 'small talk' and he would've popped the question!"

Laughing, they strode through the revolving doors, hand in hand. Eyes tearing from the frigid wind, Simone glanced down the street in search of their limo. "Where's the limo?"

"Don't worry. I got it covered."

"We're not walking into town, are we?"

Marcus heard the panic in her voice and hugged her to his chest. "No, tonight we're going first-class all the way."

"What's better than a stretch limo?" Simone felt a gush of cold air and spun around. A pair of black horses, each sporting a streak of white hair, galloped up the street, hauling a cozy two-seater sleigh. To her surprise, the animals pulled up to her smoothly and their ruddy-cheeked owner tipped his cap in greeting.

"Your chariot awaits," Marcus said with a flourish of his hand.

Beyond shocked, Simone took a moment to gather herself. Closing her open mouth, she glanced from her husband to the horses and back again. Over the years, Marcus had taken her on limousine and helicopter rides, but nothing compared to this. Blown away by the romantic gesture, Simone couldn't find the words to express how she was feeling inside.

The slow, peaceful trek from the base of the Chateau up the winding trail offered a stunning view. A blustery northern wind whipped through the trees, and when the horses jerked to the left, Simone feared the sleigh might tip over. High, thin clouds covered the sky like a veil and the half-moon was flanked by dozens of stars. Snow-blanketed hills, towering meadows and the peaceful sounds of nature created an intoxicating backdrop.

Being in the carriage, surrounded by the soaring mountains, made Simone feel at one with nature and closer to Marcus than ever before. Snug in her husband's arms, she relished the beauty of the moment. *I could stay like this forever.*

Wishing it weren't so cold, Marcus picked up one of the mink blankets provided and spread it over Simone's shoulders. They shared a smile as he cradled her against his chest. Holding his wife in his arms made him feel strong, powerful, alive. Life was perfect. He had a successful business, two great sons and the love and support of his wife. Simone was the coolest, sexiest woman he had ever known, and although they butted heads from time to time, he couldn't imagine his life without her. His appetite for her was endless, beyond his control, and when she parted her lips, inviting his kiss, he crushed his mouth against her soft lips.

Simone closed her eyes, submitted to the desperate urgency of his kiss. Her fingertips were numb, but as Marcus stroked the length of her neck and shoulders, her body warmed from the inside out. Desire sparked, grew, filled her from head to toe.

The sleigh stopped.

"We're here," Marcus announced, slowly relinquishing his hold.

Simone opened her eyes and blinked into focus. "Here where?"

"I remember a certain someone saying she'd *love* to have Cajun food tonight."

Pleased that he'd remembered, Simone squeezed the hand he offered and stepped down from the sleigh. *God, I love this man!* Underneath his leather jacket, he was sporting a chocolate-brown sweater, dark slacks and casual shoes. Her husband smelled good, looked good and had the confidence of an Oscar winner. He'd stepped up his game tonight, and Simone couldn't wait to see what other surprises he had up his sleeve.

At the entrance of the Jazz Bar and Grill, they were greeted by the manager and ushered past the waiting area to the chef's table. There, they sampled crab cakes and watched the head chef flambé their main course. The succulent aroma rising from the stove filled the air. Simone felt ravenous, so downright hungry she wanted to grab a fork and dig right in.

"We should just eat here," Marcus joked, eyeballing the whiskey-drenched beef.

Simone agreed. "I can already taste it in my mouth—"

Cheers, laughter and whistles erupted behind her.

"It sounds like that's the place to be." Marcus pointed his wine flute at the crowd at the adjacent bar. "Are they watching hockey?"

The manager nodded. "It's usually not this rowdy in here, but our local team is playing, and everyone came out to cheer them on."

"Then we definitely won't be eating near the bar," Simone quipped, "because once my husband starts watching hockey he forgets all about me!"

Marcus chuckled, hung his head. "Guilty as charged."

Everyone laughed.

"I have the perfect spot for you," the manager said, gesturing to the revolving doors. "It's secluded, private and far away from the crowd."

Simone smiled. "I love it already!"

To escape the noise and gaiety of the crowd, the manager led them into a private elevator that carried them to the second-floor dining room. Inviting and natural, the hushed lighting, soothing teal paint and tall, wingback chairs gave the intimate space a classic, old-world feel. The instrumental music playing created a romantic mood, one that inspired Simone to wrap her arms around her husband's waist. "I can't believe we have this whole floor to ourselves."

"This space is reserved for special occasions and must be booked three months in advance," the manager explained. "But, like I told your husband when he called, any friend of Angela Kelly is a friend of mine."

"How do you know Angela?" Simone asked, surprised by his announcement.

"I've known Ms. Kelly for years. Thanks to the story she did on uninsured women battling breast cancer, my daughter was able to get the lifesaving treatment she needed for free. Cicelia has been in remission for six years now, but not a day goes by that I don't think about the compassion and selflessness of Angela Kelly." He coughed, blinked back the tears that filled his eyes. "Next time you see her give her a great, big ol' hug for me, okay?"

Simone nodded. "Will do."

A petite waitress, decked out in an orange football jersey, arrived carrying a tray filled with drinks, appetizers and entrees. After serving the food, the waitress lowered the music, lit the cinnamon-scented candles positioned around the room and then departed with her boss.

Alone now, Marcus reached across the booth and stroked Simone's arm. "You're cold."

"Freezing's more like it," she confessed, rubbing her hands together under the cozy, circular table. To please Marcus, she'd bought the clingy designer dress, but there was nothing cute about shivering, and if Simone could change into something else, she would. "This is what I get for wearing a minidress in the middle of winter."

"I love that dress. It shows off your cleavage and those

killer curves of yours." Grinning from ear to ear, Marcus slipped out of the booth and settled down in the seat beside her. "Don't sweat it, baby. I'll have you warmed up in no time."

A giggle tickled the back of Simone's throat. And when Marcus nibbled on her earlobe, she shrieked. The deadly combination of his cologne, his tongue and the dulcet sound of his whisper made her head spin and her body quiver with an overwhelming sense of need.

"Better?" he asked, caressing her thighs. "All warm and cozy now?"

"Yeah, but we can't sit like this all night."

"Why not?" He dropped a kiss on her lips, tightened his hold around her waist. "We're the only ones up here. We can do *anything* we want, and once our waitress drops off dessert, I'm giving her the rest of the night off!"

While J. Holiday crooned about lovemaking and promises of forever, Marcus and Simone fed each other, shared long kisses and admired the stunning mountain view. Admiring the stars in the sky from their corner booth was amazing, the single most incredible thing Simone had ever seen, and when Marcus said the view paled to her beauty, she beamed like the stars in the sky.

"You know what? I think you're right," Marcus said, putting down his fork and taking a swig of his ice water. "We should stay a few more days. I'm sure Mom wouldn't mind watching the boys a little longer. When I spoke to her this afternoon she said as much."

"We can't, Marcus. My interview is on Monday morning, remember?"

A scowl wrinkled his forehead. "I hate the idea of you working, Simone."

"Why? It's only a few hours a week."

"I know, but I want you to be free to travel with me. I love having you close by, and I'm all for mixing a little business with a *lot* of pleasure," he announced with a salacious wink. "And, I thought you wanted to get pregnant this year."

"No," she corrected, pointing a finger at him. "That's your dream, not mine. We have two great kids and that's more than enough for me."

"But you always said you wanted four or five kids."

"Yeah, that was *before* I gave birth to nine-pound twin boys!" Simone laughed and shook her head and the thought of having another child out of her mind. "As far as I'm concerned, we're done, but if I change my mind, you'll be the first to know."

"We're not done, not even close," he whispered, slipping a hand under her dress and brushing his fingertips against the front of her satin thong panties. "I'm just getting started, baby, so sit back and enjoy the ride...."

Chapter 12

"Tell me what you want...." Marcus ordered, capturing her earlobe between his teeth.

"I want you to...to...stop," she lied, ignoring the tingling sensation pulsing in her core. "The restaurant's packed. Someone could walk in on us."

"Then I better make this quick."

Simone pressed a hand to his chest to stop the sensual assault, but as he loved and caressed her with his lips, she couldn't think of anything she wanted more than to make love. Here. Now. With the cheers of the patrons downstairs playing in the background.

Marcus delved between her legs. Parting her lips with his thumb, he stroked and massaged her clit with expert precision.

"Oh, my... Yeah, baby, that's it...that's my spot!"

Simone sucked in a breath, gripped the side of the table so she wouldn't slide to the floor. His stroke was urgent. Intense. Out of this world. The single best thing to happen to Simone since Spanx were invented. The muscles between her legs quivered, contracted.

To increase the intensity of her orgasm, Simone rocked against his fingers, swirling and spinning her hips at breakneck speed. A groan blasted out of her mouth with the force of a bomb shooting out of a cannon. They came together for a kiss. One laced with hunger and a dizzying blend of passion, need and lust. When they finally came up for air, Simone had a glazed, faraway look in her eyes. And when Marcus eased another finger inside her, diving straight into her G-spot, she oohed and cooed and ahhed.

Opening her legs wider, Simone leaned forward in her seat and rested her body against the table. Thank God it wasn't made of glass. With all the rocking and bucking she was doing, it would have shattered into a million pieces.

His lips grazed her cheek, caused desire to whip through her flesh and mingle with the shivers shooting down her spine. A fast, hard orgasm—one as powerful as a ten-foot tidal wave—slammed into her, stealing her breath.

Seconds later, her legs stopped shaking, her vision cleared and she reclaimed her voice. Lowering her head, she covered her face with her hands. They were alone, safe from prying eyes, but that didn't stop her cheeks from burning with embarrassment. Yesterday, they'd had sex in the limo, and tonight they'd gone at it in a five-star restaurant. What had gotten into her? When had she become a raving sex fiend with no conscience? *There must be something in the water,* she decided, dabbing at the perspiration dotting her forehead with her napkin. *Because ever since we arrived in Manchester we've been going at it like newlyweds!*

"Baby, are you okay?"

Simone nodded, waited for her mind to clear before speaking.

"I'm going to the men's room," Marcus said, giving her a quick kiss. "I'll be right back."

While he was gone, Simone composed herself. She combed errant strands of hair back into her ponytail, dabbed perfume on her neck and wrists. Straightening her dress, Simone decided there wouldn't be any more fooling about in the booth. It didn't matter that her husband's touch aroused her or that his fiery French kisses were enough to make her come. She was a wife, a mother, a social worker for goodness' sake! And the last time she checked, getting down and dirty in public was against the law.

Simone was so caught up in her thoughts, so busy berating herself for losing control—again—that she didn't realize Marcus had returned until she felt his hand on her shoulder.

"We better get going, baby."

"But we haven't had dessert."

"Oh, yes, we did," he argued, a devilish gleam in his eyes. "It just wasn't on a plate."

The heat coursing through Simone's body torched her cheeks.

"Now, let's get out of here before I bend you over the table and have my way with you."

I wish you would, Simone thought, taking the hand he offered. *Having sex in public is wrong, but that sounds like one delicious threat!*

Downstairs, Marcus squared the bill, thanked the manager and checked out the score of the game. As they exited the restaurant, he hooked an arm around Simone's waist, held her close. They wandered around the downtown streets, staring into store windows, sharing kisses under the lampposts, reveling in the calm of the crisp winter night.

"How am I doing so far? Are you having a good time?" Marcus asked, squeezing her hand.

"I'm having the best time. I never imagined we could have this much fun in Manchester, but you were right, it's a very charming place."

"Ready for more?"

"As long as it includes getting into a cab!" she joked, snuggling her face into the arm of his jacket. "These stiletto boots are all the rage this season, but they're killing my feet!"

Chuckling, he dropped a kiss on her cheek. "Hang in there, baby. We're almost there."

"Almost where?"

"You'll see. Trust me, you won't be disappointed."

Marcus was right. Not only did Simone let out a squeal when they arrived at the Magic Ice Festival, she whipped out her cell phone and snapped dozens of pictures of the frozen, life-size sculptures. Every winter, Manchester hosted the World Art Championships, and the one-week event attracted artists, international tourists and outdoor enthusiasts from around the globe. Created with thousands of pounds of ice and dramatic colored lights each structure stood over ten feet tall and contained intricate, elaborate designs.

Holding hands, they strode through the magnificent, block-long exhibit. They stopped to pose for pictures, bought cappuccinos from the street vendor and cuddled to stay warm.

"Do you want to check out the castle?" Simone asked, pointing up the long, narrow road. "I overheard a kid say it's the best sculpture here."

Marcus checked his watch. "We better not. The concert starts in ten minutes and it's going to take us about that long to get there."

"What concert?"

"I didn't tell you?" He wore a surprised face, but his lips were twitching, and there was a stroke of humor in his tone. "Faith Evans is performing tonight at the civic center. One night only and I got us front-row seats."

"Get out!" Simone shrieked, jumping into his arms. "You're kidding me!"

"Would I joke about something as serious as that? I know how much you love her, and when I found out she was in town, I bought us tickets."

"You're kidding!"

"Babe, you said that already." Marcus chuckled and hugged her to his chest. "Why do you look so surprised? I told you this was going to be a special weekend for us, didn't I?"

"I know, it's just…" she trailed off, shook her head.

"It's just what?"

"This is all too much. The carriage ride, dinner and now we're going to a concert. I'm feeling a little nostalgic," Simone confessed, thoughts of the night they met filling her mind. "It's like our first date all over again."

Wearing a broad, I'm-the-man grin, Marcus pressed his lips to her temple. "The best is yet to come, baby. Just wait until you see what I have planned for tomorrow!"

"Slow down, Marcus," Simone cautioned, raising her voice above the clamor in the overcrowded hotel café. "Your food's not running away!"

Chuckling heartily, Marcus reached out, plucked a hash brown off her plate and tossed it into his open mouth. Sitting at one of the back tables, on cushy, high-backed seats, not only gave the couple privacy, but it put them an arm's length away from the breakfast buffet. The scent of coffee brewing and bacon sizzling made Simone think of home. And though she'd spoken to Jayden and Jordan a couple hours ago, she missed them dearly and wondered if they were having fun tobogganing with their cousins.

"These ham-and-cheese crepes are out of this world. I don't know about you, but I'm definitely having seconds."

"Now I know why the boys scarf down their waffles during breakfast," she teased, unable to resist poking fun at her husband. "They're imitating you!"

"I wouldn't be so hungry if you hadn't jumped me last night in the shower, then roused me awake again this morning. There must be something in the air because you've been insatiable between the sheets ever since we arrived in town…."

The warm glow of her husband's smile and his gentle caresses along her forearm put Simone in the mood—again. Grabbing her glass, she stirred her peach lemonade with a straw, then raised it to her parted lips. *If this doesn't cool me down, I don't know what will!*

Slow dancing last night at the Faith Evans concert had put Simone in the mood for lovemaking. That's why she had suggested a trip to the hotel specialty store after the concert. Inside Discreet Boutiques they'd picked up gels, lotions and a dizzying assortment of adult toys. While perusing the shelves, they'd flirted, touched and kissed, and even made out in one of the changing rooms. Back inside their cabin, Marcus had fulfilled her every desire, every spoken and unspoken wish, and when Simone finally fell asleep, it was with a dreamy smile on her lips.

"What do you want to do first?" Marcus asked, forking a heap of hash browns into his mouth. "A tour of the Music Hall of Fame Museum or hit the slopes?"

"Let's go to the museum. I looked it up online, and it's one of the most popular tourist attractions in the world. I'm really excited to check it out."

"Me, too, but after what you did to me in bed this morning, I can barely move."

Showers of sunshine streamed through the tall, curved windows. Falling across Marcus's face, they illuminated the mischievous twinkle in his piercing deep brown eyes.

Wearing a saucy smile, she leaned forward until their lips were just a kiss away. "For the rest of the trip, I'll keep my hands to myself. Okay?"

"Sure you will." Marcus pulled up the bottom of his shirt and exposed his chiseled, rock-hard chest. "We both know you can't live without all of this."

Simone giggled and shook her head when he started posing and profiling. Standing, she wiped her hands on a napkin and dropped it on her plate. "I'm going to the ladies' room."

Marcus captured her arm, pulled her to him. "You know, I've always fantasized about sexin' you in a men's washroom...."

"Then you better buy your own restaurant!"

The couple shared a laugh, then a kiss that made Simone feel light on her feet.

While Marcus waited, he checked his email from his phone. It rang, and when Nate's number filled the screen, he debated taking the call. Nate had been blowing up his phone all weekend, and Marcus suspected he was in trouble. Gambling was his buddy's Achilles' heel, and although his fiancée had dumped him over his boozing, partying ways, he refused to give it up. On the third ring, Marcus hit the talk button and put the phone to his ear. "Hey, man, what's up?"

"You're alive?"

Marcus chuckled. "I came up to Manchester to meet with the executives from Health Plus, remember? I told you all about it last week."

"My bad, bro. I've been so busy at the downtown location that I forgot."

"It's cool. We'll be back in a few days."

The waiter came, refilled his glass and rushed off.

"You'll never guess who called yesterday," Nate said. "Coach Strickland."

"I haven't talked to him in ages. How's the old man doing?"

"Good, he needs a favor."

"Lay it on me."

"The guest speaker booked for Career Week canceled at the last minute, and he wants you to step in. The university is willing to pay you handsomely to do it, too."

Marcus's jaw hit the table with a thud. "For real?"

"Yup, and that's not the best part. They've lined up radio and TV interviews, and in true University of Atlanta fashion, they're promoting the hell out of the event."

Adrenaline shot through his veins, creating the ultimate high. What an honor! He was going to be the guest speaker for Career Week, one of the biggest events of the year at his alma mater. Smiling wide and bright, he rocked eagerly back and forth in his seat. He'd finally made it. Arrived. Made something of himself. This invitation proved it, and Marcus was so pumped up, so excited, he felt like doing backflips around the room.

"Sign me up. I'll do anything for Coach. If he hadn't gone to bat for me back in the day, I never would have graduated!"

Nate chuckled and admitted that Coach Strickland had saved his neck a time or two. "Career Week starts tomorrow, so you guys need to head to Atlanta tonight."

Marcus groaned. "I should have known this was too good to be true."

"But I thought you loved Atlanta."

"I do, but—"

"But what? The ATL is a hell of a lot better than Manchester, and it's warmer, too!"

Returning to the table, Simone sat down in her chair, picked up her fork and selected a piece of heart-shaped fruit from the ceramic dessert bowl.

"Later, man," Marcus said, anxious to wrap up his call and share his good news with Simone. "Text me all the necessary information."

"Will do. See you in the ATL, bro!"

Ending his call, he set his cell phone on the table. "That was Nate."

"I figured as much. What does he want?" Simone smirked, raised her index finger in the air. "Let me guess. He wants to take the boys out for lunch so he can score some chicks."

Marcus winced. "Ouch, that's cold."

"What? You don't think he offers to babysit out of the goodness of his heart do you?"

The couple laughed.

"This is so good," Simone gushed, dipping a piece of kiwi into the homemade chocolate sauce. "I better stop eating this before I split the zipper on my skinny jeans!"

Chuckling, Marcus watched his wife quickly devour the bowl of fruit. Her eyes were bright, her flawless brown skin was glowing and an indulgent smile sat on her rosy-pink lips. She was in a great mood, obviously looking and feeling on top of the world, and when he told her they were headed for Atlanta, she would probably leap into his arms. *And Simone thinks I'm not romantic,* he thought, indulging in a proud grin. *Little does she know, I'm the man!*

"Guess who has been invited to give the opening address at Career Week for U of A?" Marcus asked, popping the collar on his casual, button-down shirt. "He's handsome, successful and one hell of a kisser...."

Simone choked on the piece of kiwi inside her mouth, felt it lodge painfully in the back of her throat. Or maybe it was the shock of her husband's announcement that made her eyes burn with tears. The last thing Marcus needed was another job to add to his already busy schedule, but since Simone didn't want to rain on his parade she found a smile and pasted it on her lips. "Congratulations," she said with false enthusiasm. "That's awesome. I'm so proud of you."

"So, you're okay with me cutting our romantic weekend short."

"You are? Why?"

"Career Week starts tomorrow, and I need to meet with the organizers tonight," Marcus explained, glancing down at his phone. "I'm just waiting for Nate to text me the travel itinerary."

Her eyebrows jammed together, formed a crooked, angry line. "But what about our trip to the museum, the winery and the dinner theater show tomorrow night?"

"I'll make it up to you. I promise."

Simone couldn't believe it. Marcus was bailing on her—again. But this time, he was leaving her alone, in a cold, frigid city that was thousands of miles away from home. "So, that's it. You're just going to leave me here and head off to Atlanta with Nate?"

"Of course not, baby. I'm taking you with me." Marcus winked and caressed the length of her forearm. "I need you to keep me warm at night."

"But I don't want to waste the whole day flying to Atlanta. I want to stay here."

Concealing his disappointment, he lifted his glass to his

mouth and tasted his drink. Marcus wanted Simone by his side when he addressed the sophomore class, wanted her to hear him publicly declare that she and the boys were the best thing that ever happened to him, the true driving force behind his success. But instead of begging her to reconsider, he tried to lighten the mood, and joked, "You must *really* want to sample the new stock at the winery."

Simone didn't laugh. "I really miss the boys," she said, putting down her fork and scrubbing at the sauce staining her fingers with one of the cherry-red napkins provided. "I should just go home and spend the rest of the weekend with them."

Marcus nodded. What else could he do? Get down on his knees and say, "I want you by my side, so please, baby, please, come with me to Atlanta?" Giving his head a hard shake cleared his thoughts and made him realize the only way to come out on top of this conversation was by agreeing with her. "You're right. You should."

"You have some nerve."

His grin froze on his face.

"I thought you were trying to change, but I was wrong. You're just as selfish as ever!"

"Simone, keep your voice down."

Her eyes narrowed into a hideous glare. "Don't tell me what to do."

"You're making a scene."

"I'm making a scene," she stammered. "Well, you're being a...a...a...jerk!"

"A jerk?" Marcus jabbed a finger at his chest. "Are you kidding me? Do you have any idea how much money I've spent this weekend?"

"Oh, please. Don't make it sound like you planned this trip for me. You had business meetings here, remember? I just tagged along."

"You're right," he conceded with a nod of his head. "I did come down here for business, but the best part of this weekend has been being with you. Laughing, joking, staying up late into the night talking and making love."

Right. That's why you're leaving. To keep from unleashing her full fury on Marcus, Simone clamped her lips together and counted to ten. It didn't help to calm her. Anger rose inside her, consumed her. Every time they made a little progress, they hit another bump in the road, and Simone was sick of Marcus ditching her. Work came first, and she came last. That's the way it had always been. Likely the way it would stay unless she took a stand now. "*You* promised there'd be no interruptions this weekend," she said, unable to hold her tongue. "*You* said this weekend was all about us, remember? Or have you conveniently forgotten now that something more important has come up?"

"Wow, if I knew you would get this upset, I never would have agreed to go to Atlanta."

Staring at him, wide-eyed and openmouthed, Simone listened in stunned disbelief as he accused her of being melodramatic. It took every ounce of her self-control to keep from kicking him in the shin. His insults stabbed her ears, made them ache and throb.

"Why are you getting all riled up? It's not that serious. If you want me to stay, I'll stay. No need to get hysterical."

"Don't do me any favors," she spat. "I couldn't care less whether you stay or go."

A brief look of sadness passed over his features. "Fine, then I'll leave tonight."

"Why wait? I bet you could get a flight within the hour."

"I just might do that."

Angry enough to spit fire, Simone pushed back her chair and grabbed her purse. She heard her cell phone ring but ignored it.

"Where are you going? We're not finished eating."

"You're not, but I am."

In her haste to leave, Simone bumped the table and knocked over her glass. Peach lemonade flowed over the table like a mighty rushing river, and when Marcus jumped to his feet, an aghast expression on his face, she felt the impulse to laugh. But there was nothing funny about the way he'd spoken to her or his decision to end their trip early. Or the fact that he spent little time with their sons, but had all the time in the world to meet with his celebrity clients and business associates.

Moving faster than a professional speed walker, Simone stormed out of the dining room, through the restaurant and into the waiting elevator. The doors slid closed, sealing her inside the metal box with two burly men sporting cowboy hats. Simone felt tears dribbling down her cheeks, and turned her face toward the wall.

Forget Marcus. Forget bending over backward to make him happy. Tired of playing second fiddle to his career, Simone decided right then and there to stop catering to him. From now on, she was doing her own thing. Look out for numero uno. And her first order of business was to get a job. She'd show him! She'd have a successful career, and places to go and people to see, too. Let's see how Marcus liked being—

Hearing her cell phone, Simone slid her hands inside her purse and pulled it out. Once she checked the number on the screen and saw that it wasn't Marcus, she answered. "I'm sorry I didn't get to call you back last night," Simone said to Angela, stepping off the elevator and flopping onto one of the chairs outside of the hotel spa. "We returned late from dinner."

"No worries, girl. I was just calling to see how you guys were doing and to remind you to pick up a bottle of merlot for me when you go to the winery this afternoon."

"We're not going."

Angela sounded as if she was grinning. "Having too much fun to leave the cabin, huh?"

"We *were,* until Marcus had to go and ruin our romantic weekend." Simone told Angela everything, and when she was done, she was even more upset. "We were having such a good time, and now I'm so angry and frustrated all I want to do is go home."

"I'm almost as mad as you are," Angela said, raising her voice. "It wasn't easy getting you guys a cabin at Chateau LeBlanc, and I had to pull a lot of strings to get those tickets to the dinner theater show. Geesh! All that hard work for nothing."

Simone blinked and stared down at the phone. "You planned our trip?"

Silence plagued the line. Then, after what seemed like hours, Angela spoke. "Marcus asked what I thought you'd like to do, and I gave him some suggestions."

"Yeah, which he followed to the tee," Simone said, sinking further into the abyss of despair and disappointment. "I can't believe you let him trick you into planning our trip."

"He didn't trick me." A pause, then, "I prefer to think of it as exchanging services. Marcus put me in touch with the GM of the Chicago Bears for my piece on athletes behaving badly, and in exchange I gave him a list of things to do and see in Manchester."

Simone blinked back hot tears. Could this day get any worse? Breathing deeply through her nose, she touched a hand to her neck. It felt like someone had poured hot sauce down her throat. Her mouth burned, and her throat felt so tight and constricted, she feared she'd choke.

"Where's Marcus now?"

"Don't know, don't care."

"Do you want me to meet you in Manchester?"

Choked up, Simone stumbled over her words. "Y-You'd do that for me?"

"Of course, we're girls! I've got your back, and you've got mine."

"Thanks for offering, but I think I'm going to head home."

Angela sighed in relief. "Thank God! I hate Manchester in the winter, and I don't have a gorgeous man like you do to keep me warm on those cold, frigid nights."

"You're better off having no man than being with someone who leaves you at the drop of a dime." Simone stared down at her hands and slid her wedding ring absently up and down her finger. She spotted Dr. RaShondra's book poking out of her purse and grunted so loud she startled the Asian woman exiting the spa. "I can't believe I wasted my time and money reading *A Sista's Guide to Seduction*. I implemented the rules, but Marcus is *still* blowing me off."

"I told you that book was silly, but you wouldn't listen."

"Way to kick a girl when she's down," Simone quipped, sighing in frustration.

"You know who you need? Jaxson Stafford."

"Who's that?"

"He's a successful attorney with a background in psychology who also specializes in couple's therapy. I interviewed him last year, and not only is he fine as hell, he's smart and intelligent and incredibly knowledgeable about family law. I'll give you his card the next time I see you. Hey—" she yelled with more pep than a high school cheerleader "—why don't you come over? I don't have sexy dimples or a wicked set of abs like that gorgeous husband of yours, but I'm free tonight."

A giggle broke free from Simone's pursed lips. "You are too crazy."

"I know, that's why you love me! So, it's all set. I'll pick you up at the airport, and you'll spend the night."

"I'd be terrible company, and besides, I really should go get the boys."

"Girl, please, they're having so much fun they're not even thinking about you!"

"Remind me *not* to call you the next time I'm having a bad day."

"Oh, hush," Angela ordered, though her tone was warm with humor. "And quit being so sour while you're at it. It'll be fun! We'll make popcorn, watch movies and…"

Staring down at her hands, Simone reflected on the last three weeks. She'd been following the tips in the little pink book faithfully, but using sex to get Marcus's attention clearly wasn't working. Sure, they were having fun, but they didn't have the deep, emotional bond she longed for. If they did, he wouldn't be cutting their trip short to head off to Atlanta."I'm just not in the mood to hang out," she said. "I just want to be alone."

"But I have a tub of cookie dough, double-fudge brownies and two bottles of sambuca chilling in the fridge just for you. And while we're pigging out, we can talk about ways to get your marriage back on track."

Simone loved the sound of that. She needed all the help she could get to improve her relationship, and she knew her best friend would come up with great ideas. Standing, she frantically jabbed at the elevator button. "Don't start without me!" she said with a laugh. "I'll call you when I reach the airport!"

Chapter 13

Simone closed the dishwasher, pressed the start button and wiped down the appliances. Surveying the room, her gaze carefully sweeping from one end to the next, she ensured that everything was in its rightful place. Pleased that the kitchen was finally spick-and-span, Simone untied her apron and dropped it on the granite counter.

Since returning home from Manchester, she'd been cleaning everything in sight. Anything to keep her mind off Marcus and the things he'd said. He was due back tonight, within the hour, and just the thought of seeing him made her stomach coil into knots. Would they talk about what happened? Or pretend nothing was wrong like they usually did?

Simone stood still for a moment, listening. She heard the television, but nothing else. It wasn't often that Jayden and Jordan occupied the same space peacefully and since she hadn't heard a peep from them since they went into the living room, she knew something was awry. Either they had snuck off to her bedroom or they were outside in the backyard eating snow.

Hurrying down the hall, as fast as her feet could take her, she called out their names. When Simone entered the living room and saw Jayden and Jordan, she stopped short. Not only were they sitting on the same couch; they were talking nicely to each other and wearing big smiles. Jayden was curled up underneath his blanket reading a book, and Jordan was playing with his toy trucks.

"How are you guys doing?"

"Good," Jordan said, glancing up from his toy bucket. "Mom, can I have some chips?"

"No, you just ate dinner."

"But I'm still hungry."

Jayden gave a vigorous nod of his head. "Me, too. I'm starving."

"Okay, then I'll bring you some grapes."

"No, thanks," Jordan replied, puckering his lips. "Just the chips."

Laughing to herself, Simone leaned over and ruffled his hair. If it wasn't salty or crunchy, Jayden wasn't interested. Watching her sons play, she wondered how anyone could ever confuse them. They dressed differently, spoke differently and had very different personalities, but just yesterday, their kindergarten teacher, Mrs. Owosu-Daniels, had confessed that after one full week of school she still couldn't tell them apart. To help her, Simone had the boys stand side by side, and pointed at their eyes. Jordan's were wide, expressive, the darkest shade of brown there was, while Jayden's were narrow and tinged with specks of gray. The first-year teacher had thanked her profusely and promised to stop mixing them up.

"I hope Daddy comes home soon," Jayden said softly. "I miss him."

So do I, Simone thought but didn't say. Every night at six o'clock, Marcus called from Atlanta to check in, and every night Simone found an excuse not to talk to him. She didn't want to rehash what happened in Manchester or argue about her new job, either. Tomorrow was her first day at Friendship House, and although she was nervous about rejoining the workforce after a five-year absence, she was excited about working at the nonprofit center. And now that Simone had reliable child care lined up for the boys, she was feeling more confident about her decision.

"Can Dad take us to play air hockey when he gets home?" Jordan smashed two trucks together, making the appropriate sound effects.

"I don't know. It's almost six-thirty and you boys have to be at school tomorrow."

"But he promised!"

"Maybe you guys can go on the weekend—"

Simone heard heavy footsteps on the hardwood floor. Jayden and Jordan scrambled to their feet and tore down the hall, laughing and shrieking as they went. The boys adored their dad, loved him more than anything in the world, and the feeling was definitely mutual. After growing up without a father, Simone often wondered how different life would be if her dad had been around. *Maybe I wouldn't depend on Marcus so much or crave his affection the way I do.*

Her gaze fell across their wedding picture proudly displayed on the mantel. To this day, no one knew that she was pregnant when they had eloped to the Dominican Republic, and whenever Simone looked at that photograph, her heart murmured a sigh of happiness. Given the chance, she'd marry Marcus all over again. He was charming and fun, attentive and loving, and although he could be insensitive at times, there was no one else she wanted to spend her life with.

"Mommy, look what Daddy bought me!" Jayden waved the *Toy Story* play pack wildly in the air. "It has glow-in-the-dark stickers and everything!"

"That's great."

"Daddy brought you something, too, Mommy. Come see!"

Simone didn't move. Not a muscle. Why should she? The last time she saw Marcus he'd been cold and condescending, and even though she'd promised herself she wouldn't bring up their argument, she was still hurt about the things he'd said.

Marcus entered the living room with shopping bags in his hands and Jordan swinging from his back, screeching like a howler monkey. "Look at me! I'm the king of the world!"

The boys cracked up.

Simone found a smile and spread it on her lips. "Hey. How are you?"

"Hey yourself. You're looking gorgeous as usual."

Marcus bent down and brushed his lips against her cheek. He made sure to rest his hand on her neck, at the spot he knew drove her wild. Simone shivered and rubbed her hands over her arms. Dammit, he looked good. Clean-shaven, tailored suit, shoes buffed to perfection and sporting that wide, boyish grin that whipped her body into a frenzy every damn time.

Simone dodged his gaze. She had to be strong, had to ignore the warmth of his silky caress along her shoulders. They had to talk, and Simone didn't want her judgment to be clouded. But once they cleared the air, there would be plenty of time for makeup sex. Because Lord knew she wanted some. Even though she was hurt about the things he'd said, she still desired him. Marcus was her dream, her world, the only man who could make her body sing, and every time he looked at her she envisioned them making sweet love.

"How was your trip?" she asked, shaking the image of his hard, naked body from her mind. "Did you have a good time at Career Week?"

"It was all right. It would've been better if you were there, though."

"Are you hungry?"

"Starving."

Running his eyes down her chest, he wet his lips with seductive flair.

Simone knew that look. Knew they weren't talking about the seafood pasta she'd made for dinner. Her husband was in the mood, raring to go, and she could almost see the sexual energy radiating off his smooth, brown skin.

"I missed you, babe. That's why I came home a couple days early."

Simone wasn't buying it. Not this time. If she was so near and dear to his heart, the woman he claimed to love, he never would have ditched her in Manchester. "I'm glad you had a safe trip. The boys have been asking about you nonstop."

"I missed these little rug rats, too."

Jordan and Jayden giggled, laughed like it was the funniest thing they'd ever heard.

"I almost forgot, these are for you." Marcus held out the shopping bags, gestured for her to take them. "I hope everything fits."

"This is a lot of stuff. What did you buy?"

"Just a few things I thought you'd like."

Simone took the bags and rested them at her feet. "Thanks."

"You're not going to open them?"

"I will, after I give the boys a bath and put them to bed."

Marcus looped an arm around Jayden's neck. "I can do it."

"Yay!" Jayden and Jordan cheered. "We can play with our bath toys!"

Simone raised an eyebrow. Her husband—the same man who'd once fainted while changing Jordan's diaper—was offering to do the dreaded bedtime routine? *Wonders never cease,* she thought, returning his smile. "Are you sure?"

"Positive. Go upstairs and unwind. I'll be up in a few."

Scared he would change his mind, Simone kissed the boys good-night, scooped up the shopping bags and hightailed it out of the room as fast as her slipper-clad feet could take her.

Ten minutes later, Simone was in the master bedroom, having a one-woman fashion show. Blouses, skirts and belts were scattered across the bed, and a half-dozen pair of designer shoes covered the carpet.

Reaching into a glitzy shopping bag, Simone took out a black one-shoulder dress and admired the flattering cut. Her eyes widened. It looked like the same dress she'd tried on at the hotel boutique in Manchester. A frown furrowed her cheeks. No way! It couldn't be!

Rummaging through the shopping bags, Simone searched and searched until she found what she was looking for. Bingo! The receipt confirmed it. Marcus *had* bought the clothes in Manchester. Simone's heart softened. *That's why I didn't see him before I left for the airport,* she thought, her mind replaying that last morning in Manchester. *I thought Marcus was avoiding me, but he was in the hotel boutique shopping.*

Simone had mixed feelings. She was flattered that Marcus had shopped for her, but she wished he had taken the time to resolve things before he left for Atlanta. After all, hadn't she told Marcus time and time again that she didn't need any more expensive gifts? All she needed was him. That was it. He was all she'd ever wanted, all she'd ever need.

"Dad, can I bring my water guns into the tub?"

"Sure, why not? We'll have a good old-fashioned shoot-out!"

Cheers filled the air.

Simone heard water running, splashing, and wondered how long and messy bath time was going to be. Marcus wouldn't be finished anytime soon, but instead of trying on the remaining items in the bags, Simone went into the bathroom.

Humming softly, she grabbed her lighter and lit the incense sticks positioned around the tub. *One good deed deserves another,* she thought, repeating her great-grandmother's favorite quote. *And after we smooth everything over, I'm going to put* it *on him!*

Marcus flew up the staircase. Breathing heavily, like a thief running from the law, he charged into the master bedroom in search of his wife. He saw the light on in the bathroom, knew she was probably luxuriating in the tub and stripped off his clothes, one designer layer at a time.

After putting Jayden and Jordan to bed, he'd gone into the

kitchen to grab a bite to eat. But when he smelled incense burning and heard jazz music playing, he'd abandoned his food.

Loosening his tie, he unbuttoned his dress shirt and kicked off his shoes. The air was perfumed with a rich, fragrant scent, and it brought to mind their luxurious suite at the Chateau LeBlanc. Marcus dragged a hand down his face and shook his head. Leaving Simone at the resort was a mistake, no, a boneheaded thing to do. He had to make it up to her, had to show her how sorry he was, how bad he felt.

Cracking open the bathroom door, Marcus stood there for a moment, watching her. Simone had bubbles up to her neck, an expression of pure contentment on her face and a piece of fruit between her lips. Two glasses of wine and a bowl of chocolate-covered strawberries sat on the ledge. But it wasn't the tantalizing aromas in the air that made his mouth wet, it was the sight of his wife, looking sexy and delectable. "Is there room for me?"

"Always," she said in a sensuous voice.

Water splashed onto the bath mat when he sat down in the warm, soapy water. *Ah, this is the life.* Teddy Pendergrass was playing, infecting the room with his rich, soul-stirring vocals and creating a romantic mood. Streaks of moonlight coursed through the windows, showering the bathroom with a golden-white light. Stretched out, Marcus felt the tension in his shoulders and lower back float away like the bubbles surrounding him.

Leaning forward, he drew his fingertips in a gentle caress along her arm. Her head was back, resting against the tile wall, but he saw her quick intake of breath. Stroking Simone's hands wasn't enough. He wanted to feel her warmth, her closeness, wanted to run his fingers through her long, silky hair. Marcus cupped her face, cradled it in his hands like it was the Hope Diamond. "I shouldn't have gone to Atlanta."

"You're right. You shouldn't have."

"You're not going to make this easy for me, huh?"

Simone shook her head, but a smile warmed her lips.

"What do you think of the outfits? They're a peace offering. My way of saying sorry about what happened in Manchester."

"I know. I love everything you bought, but I wish you had talked to me instead of going shopping. I need you, Marcus, just you, not shoes or bags or dresses."

Nodding, he brushed his thumb slowly across her cheeks. He planted soft, light kisses on her flesh. Her lips curled into a dreamy smile, and when he sucked her earlobe into his mouth, a purr fell from her mouth. "It looks like I'm going to have to call in sick tomorrow," he announced, flashing a dirty little grin, "because I plan to make love to you all night long."

"Is that right?"

"It sure is. Your ass is mine for the next twenty-four hours!" Marcus rubbed his hands over her shoulders, stroking her skin the way she liked. "After I drop the boys off at school we'll spend the rest of the day in bed—"

"I start work tomorrow, remember?"

Marcus furrowed his eyebrows. "You took that job without discussing it with me first?"

"We did discuss it."

"And I told you I didn't like the idea of you returning to work."

Determined not to lose her cool, she straightened and took a deep breath. "Marcus, I'm only working twenty hours a week," she explained, her tone even, calm. "Nothing's going to change around here. I'll still take the boys to school every day and pick them up."

"And what happens when you have to work late?"

"Your mom offered to babysit."

Anger darkened his face. "So, everybody knows about your new job except me?"

"It's not like that," Simone argued, growing frustrated with his woe-is-me attitude. "When I picked up the kids last Sunday Gladys encouraged me to bring them over more. And—" she stressed, leaning heavily on the word "—she promised to follow the schedule, too! Only time will tell, but your mom seemed really sincere."

"You're always complaining about how busy you are, so why get a job?"

Simone paused, trying to think of a fitting rebuttal. Nothing came to mind. Working part-time was going to disrupt their family, but she loved the idea of helping abused women get back on their feet and finally putting her social work degree to good use. "I'm prepared to do whatever it takes to make this work, even if it means losing sleep or ditching my early morning classes." Simone laughed and added, "Actually, I'd love to skip Hot Yoga. That class is a killer!"

"I can't believe you."

Her laughter dried up. "You can't believe *me?*"

"We agreed that you'd resume your career once we were finished having kids, but now you're dead set against having another child. Isn't expanding our family more important than taking some crummy, low-paying job?"

Leaping out of the tub, Simone snatched a towel off the metal rack and swathed it around her waist. Gritting her teeth, she listened in steely silence as Marcus argued his point. Anger gained control of her mouth, and if not for fear of waking up the boys, she would have lashed back in high definition. Cutting him off midword, she accused him of being a hypocrite.

"It's not about the money, it's about doing something I love. Isn't that what you're always telling me?" she jeered, throwing his words back in his face. "Isn't that why you still train your celebrity clients, why you applied for that job with the Chicago Bears and the reason why you left me high and dry in Manchester—"

"Oh, *that's* what this is about. You accepted that case manager position to stick it to me."

"That's ridiculous. I applied for the job weeks ago."

"Sure you did," he drawled, his tone dripping with sarcasm.

"To get back at me for ending our trip early, you accepted that job knowing full well I don't want you to work."

"This isn't about you, Marcus. It's about me doing something I love...."

Marcus tuned out. Given the chance, Simone could spend hours on end talking about the families she counseled. As a child raised in poverty himself, he appreciated the care and concern she showed to those in need, but he wasn't behind her decision. Chicago's South Side was no place for Simone to be during the day, let alone after dark. And in no time her twenty-hour week would be a sixty-hour workweek. He'd seen it happen to his friends' wives, and he didn't want it happening to Simone. No, he wasn't going to let that happen.

"Counseling others makes me feel alive, like I'm making a difference," she confessed. "Next to being a wife and mother, it's the best job in the world, the only thing I've ever wanted to do."

Closing his open mouth, he swallowed his stinging retort. Marcus didn't speak. What could he say? He'd married a caring, compassionate woman who lived to help others, a woman who'd do anything for someone in need. Just like his mom. Gladys had worked two, sometimes three jobs just to make ends meet, and she routinely went without so that he and his siblings didn't have to. Marcus never forgot seeing his mother struggle, or the pain of being shuffled back and forth between babysitters. He didn't want that life for his sons. He didn't tell Simone the truth—that her working outside the home shattered his image of the perfect family. No, he couldn't do that. Mustering his enthusiasm, he said what any loving husband would say. "Congratulations on the new job, Simone." His voice sounded hollow, and the stiffness of his tone betrayed his true feelings. "If returning to work makes you happy, then I won't stand in your way."

"How noble of you," she mumbled, rolling her eyes.

"Whatever. Just take the job. The boys and I can manage without you."

Simone opened her mouth and spoke so calmly, so quietly, she didn't recognize her own voice. "These days, all we seem to do is argue and fight, and I'm getting tired of it," she said. "Maybe it would help if we talked to someone. Angela told me about a really great—"

He cut in. "I'm not interested in seeing a shrink."

"Why not?"

"Because, they're just as messed up as the people they counsel."

An awkward silence fell between them. It lasted for several long, painful seconds.

"I better get ready for bed," Simone finally said. "I have a long day ahead of me tomorrow, and I'm so nervous, I don't know how I'm ever going to fall asleep."

"You'll be fine, Simone. Friendship House is lucky to have you."

"Are you coming to bed soon?"

"Yeah, in a minute."

Dropping her towel in the clothes hamper, she sauntered into the bedroom, au naturel.

"Great, just great," he grumbled under his breath. "She's returning to work." He sat there, in the cool, soapy water, watching Simone move around the master bedroom. Marcus wanted to go to her, wanted to sweep her up into her arms and carry her to bed, but he couldn't stop thinking about what she'd said. Her words swirled around his head. Simone was right. There was no reason to worry. No reason to stress.

Marcus tried to block out the voices inside his head, but they continued, persisted, pursued him like an emotional stalker. *Family comes first, always has, always will,* he told himself, gaining strength from his thoughts. Simone promised nothing was going to change. *But if that's true,* he thought, watching his wife slip into a slinky, purple negligee, *then why do I have a sickening feeling that life as I know it is over?*

Chapter 14

"Does the TV have to be so loud?" Simone asked, raising her voice above the noise. She had a vegetable tray in one hand and a juice pitcher in the other, but she strode into the living room at breakneck speed. Her husband's friends were coming over to watch the big football game, and she still had a million things to do before they arrived. "Turn the volume down, Marcus. The surround sound is deafening!"

Pointing the remote at the entertainment unit, he decreased the volume and then strolled over to the glass serving table. "My friends aren't going to eat this stuff," he said, pointing at the finger foods. "We're watching a game, not the Macy's Day Parade!"

Simone patted his chest. "Don't worry, baby. I'll bring out the 'real food' once everybody gets here."

"That's my girl! You had me worried there for a second."

"And you've had me worried all day!"

Marcus chuckled. "I know I get a little crazy on game day, but I can't help it. I love college football, and my team is the favorite to win."

"Look at us, Mom and Dad. We're superheroes!" Jordan and Jayden raced into the room, giggling uncontrollably and waving toy swords in their little hands. "I'm Motorcycle Man and Jayden's Crybaby Boy."

"I don't want to be Crybaby Boy!" Pouting, Jayden chucked his sword on the floor and crossed his arms across his chest. "I want to be Motorcycle Man!"

"Boys, you can't play in here, I'm busy getting—" The rest of Simone's sentence fell away when she realized what her sons were using as face masks. She snatched her lace underwear off Jayden's head and then went after Jordan, who took off running. Once Simone retrieved her panties and stuffed them inside her apron pocket, she scolded the boys for playing in her bedroom. "Where did you get Mommy's pant—" Her voice faltered and she tripped over the word. Clearing her throat, she rephrased the question and tried again. "Where did you get those masks from?"

Jayden pointed a finger at Jordan, and Simone shot her son a stern look.

"I found them under the bed."

"Whose bed?"

"Yours." Jordan lowered his eyes to the floor, but the grin on his face remained. "There's lots of masks under your bed, and in different colors and sizes, too!"

Marcus burst out laughing. Jordan and Jayden broke free from their mother's grasp and raced over to their dad. Marcus picked them up and spun them around the living room. "Who's ready to watch football?"

Jordan cheered and Jayden moaned.

"Daddy, I don't want to watch football. I want to paint."

"Paint?" Marcus rubbed his stubbly chin across Jayden's face and he squealed in delight. "What am I going to do with you, boy?"

"Me next, Dad! Make me laugh, too!" Jordan chimed in. "Come on, Dad. Do it to me!"

The doorbell rang, and the trio set off down the hall. For

the next hour, Marcus and the boys manned the door while Simone worked in the kitchen. The serving table was covered with a wide assortment of foods, the air was filled with a tantalizing aroma and the mood in the house was festive. Simone loved entertaining, and it was the first time since starting her new job three weeks ago that she and Marcus were laughing and joking with each other.

"Hello! Welcome to our home!" Simone waved in greeting at each new arrival—even Marcus's loudmouth brother, Derek—but got so caught up frying the samosas, she didn't notice Gladys had entered the kitchen until her mother-in-law was standing right beside her. "Gladys, what are you doing here?" she asked, glancing over her shoulder. "I wasn't expecting to see you today."

"I don't see why not. I came to hang out with my grandbabies." Gladys put the white ceramic bowl she was holding down on the counter and draped her red, belted coat on one of the raised stools. "You look like you could use some help. What do you want me to do?"

"Nothing, I'm fine," Simone chirped, turning off the stove and wiping her hands on the side of her apron. "Why don't you go in the living room and relax with the other guests?"

"Because I'm not a guest. I'm family."

Don't remind me.

"See, that's your problem right there," Gladys griped, wagging a finger at her. "You think you're Wonder Woman and can do everything all by yourself."

"Calm down, Gladys. There's nothing to get upset about. All I said was—"

"Don't patronize me!" Her eyebrows jammed together, and a scowl crimped her lips. "That's why I hardly come over here anymore. I can't deal with your holier-than-thou attitude, and neither can the rest of the family. That's why we stay away."

"I don't have an attitude."

"Yes, you do," she shot back. "But what you need to do is

get a life and quit nagging my son for trying to provide for his family."

"Excuse me?"

Gladys propped a hand on her hip. "You heard me. Find something meaningful to do with your time besides sitting around all day waiting for Marcus to get home. You'll be a lot happier, and so will your family."

Simone cleared her throat. Her mother-in-law was blunt and to the point, and her words stung. Her rebuke was hard to take, but Simone wanted to improve her marriage and it started with making peace with Gladys. "I don't mean to be difficult, and I'm sorry if I ever said or did anything to offend you," she began, her voice quavering with emotion, "but sometimes I feel like you undermine me as a wife and mother."

"I would never do that," Gladys said. "I want you and Marcus and the boys to be happy. That's why I suggested you return to work, and why I offered to help out any way I can."

"I really do appreciate you helping us out with Jordan and Jayden," Simone confessed. "It's made my return to work that much easier."

"Do you like your new job?"

"I love being at Friendship House, but I'm overwhelmed by all the paperwork, and the sheer number of families I'm responsible for. There's a lot I have to learn, and right now I feel like I'm failing miserably."

"You're a smart girl. You'll get the hang of it."

The metal serving spoon in Simone's hands fell to the floor. She knew she was standing beside the stove, with her mouth wide open and a bewildered expression on her face, but she couldn't have been more stunned. "Y-y-you think I'm smart?" she stammered. "Really?"

"Of course I do! I wouldn't have encouraged my son to marry you if I didn't."

"I've always thought you didn't like me."

"You're a fabulous wife and mother, Simone, but sometimes you're too hard on my son, and it pains me to see him hurt." Her voice cracked, and her eyes began to water. For several moments she didn't speak, but when she did her tone was filled with anguish. "Marcus is a better man than his father ever was, and he loves you and the boys more than anything in the world."

Simone felt an overwhelming sense of guilt. And as she reflected quietly on what her mother-in-law said, she realized that Gladys was right. She had to stop blaming Marcus for what was wrong in their marriage and focus on all of the good things he did for their family. From now on, she was going to make a concerted effort to be more understanding. And not just with Marcus, but with the rest of his family, too. "Gladys, I love Marcus very much, and I would never do anything to hurt him. I just wish he spent more time with me and the boys, that's all."

"I can understand that," she said, nodding slowly. "But nagging never works. Remember, dear, you can catch more bees with honey than vinegar."

A smile tickled Simone's lips. She couldn't believe it. Gladys was being nice to her, and laughing and joking around, too. She stared at her mother-in-law, as if seeing her for the very first time. It felt good to confide in someone, and thanks to Gladys, she was feeling more confident not only about her job, but her abilities as a wife and mother, as well. "Thanks for the advice, Gladys. And you're right. It's time I get back to doing the things I love and quit depending on Marcus to make me happy—"

Cheers and raucous laughter filled the air, drawing Simone's attention to the living room. A gasp escaped her lips. When Marcus told her was having a "few guys" over to watch the Florida Classic, she'd offered to make dinner for the group, but Simone never imagined he'd invite dozens of people. There were bodies everywhere. On the couch, in the hallway, leaning against the living room wall. And as she watched the all-male group devour the snacks on the serving table and guzzle down the fruit punch, Simone feared she hadn't cooked enough food.

"Gladys, I think I need your help after all," Simone said, wearing an apologetic smile. "Can you grab a couple boxes of frozen lasagna and throw them into the oven?"

A smile broke out across Gladys's face. "I'd love to."

The two women worked silently, side by side, for the next forty-five minutes. Simone felt a pang in her stomach and feared she would faint if she didn't eat soon. Reaching into the ceramic bowl Gladys had brought, she swiped a Swedish meatball and popped it into her mouth. Her mother-in-law was one hell of a cook, and before Simone knew it, the bowl was half-empty. "Gladys, these meatballs are delicious!" she said, licking the sauce off her fingertips. "You have to teach me how to make them."

Gladys beamed. "It would be my pleasure."

Simone slid on her pink cooking mitts and opened the oven. The rich, mouthwatering scent that filled the air sent her stomach on a grumbling tear. She put the tray on the stove and watched as Gladys added a dash of basil to the potato skins.

"This is nice, huh? Us working together as a team."

"Thanks for all your help, Gladys. There's no way I could have cooked all of this extra food without you."

Her mother-in-law smirked. "I told you you needed my help!"

The women laughed.

"I remember how stressful it was being a working mom, so if you ever need me to take the boys to school or keep them overnight, just ask." Gladys untied her apron and dropped it on the counter. "I get lonely in that big old house by myself, and I love when Jayden and Jordan come over. They make me feel young, and laughing is the best calorie burner!"

"Then, in that case, they can spend every weekend at your house!"

Gladys gave an earnest nod, and Simone cracked up. She was so happy that they were getting along, she could have cried tears of joy. Simone didn't know if their friendship was going to last, but she sensed that this was the start of a new beginning, and she looked forward to getting to know her mother-in-law better.

"Let's make a deal," Gladys proposed, extending her right hand. "You quit acting like Wonder Woman, and I'll do a better job of sticking to that silly schedule you drew up."

Laughing, Simone shook her mother-in-law's outstretched hand. She knew Gladys would always take up for Marcus and would keep spoiling the kids, but she was glad that they had finally made peace.

"College girl, is the food ready?" Derek strolled into the kitchen, threw open the fridge and grabbed a beer. "All of the snacks are finished, and I'm starving like Marvin!"

"Here, take this." Gladys picked up the casserole dish and handed it to Simone. "Now, get out there before the men start smashing the furniture in a hungry rage!"

Taking the dish and a bottle of hot sauce, Simone set off for the living room. An army of brown-skinned men, who were smacking their lips and patting their stomachs, surrounded Simone as she arranged the food on the large serving table.

"Hi, I'm Fabian."

Simone turned to the left. A tall, lean man in a football jersey, jeans and boots was staring at her. "It's nice to meet you."

Another guy stepped forward. "I'm Bradley, but everyone calls me Tank."

"You're pretty. And, you smell good, too," a man in designer eyeglasses said.

Soon, Simone was shaking hands and engaging in small talk with everyone around the table. She panned the living room for Marcus, in the hopes that he would come rescue her from his flirtatious friends, but his eyes were glued to the big-screen TV. For all she knew, he didn't even know she was in the room. *What else is new?* she thought sadly.

"I forgot the salt and pepper." Simone spun around. "Be right back."

"That's Marcus's wife, huh?" someone said.

"Yup, that's Simone," an awe-filled voice replied. "Fine, isn't she?"

"Marcus is one lucky man."

"You can say that again."

Subduing the excitement she was feeling inside, Simone concentrated on not tripping over her feet. Dr. RaShondra said a "together woman" knew how to walk. According to the good doctor, "a together woman" moved with sinuous grace and commanded attention when she entered a room, so Simone raised her head, tilted her chin and arched her shoulders. *Tall, dark and handsome men are checking me out,* she thought, giggling. *And that's all right with me!*

Marcus stood in the middle of the living room, watching Simone. She was down on her knees, picking crumbs out of the carpet and humming softly to herself. Three weeks ago, they'd had an explosive argument in Manchester, but these days his wife was as calm as a Zen master. He had attributed her sudden nonchalant attitude and her everything's-okay smile to that pink book she was reading, but there was no book in the world that could bring about such dramatic changes in Simone's personality.

Tonight, he had witnessed firsthand just how much she had changed. When Jayden spilled grape juice on the carpet, she didn't fuss. She gave him another glass, told him to be careful and cleaned up the mess. And when Nate begged for a third helping of her famous spicy barbecue wings, she didn't roll her eyes or tell him to get lost. She smiled, took his plate and returned to the kitchen. She had done such a stellar job catering to his friends that most of the guys had shifted their attention from the game to her. At one point, he'd returned from the bathroom and found most of the guys ogling her, as she moved around the room, collecting plates and handing out cold beers. And then, there were the hungry looks and lusty smiles she received every time she bent down to pick up one of the kids' toys from off the floor.

Have I forgotten how vivacious and captivating she is? He knew Simone was special, and that he was lucky to have her, but this was the first time in months, maybe years, that he'd seen her charm a room full of men, *and* make it look easy. The desire for her was so intense, so overwhelming, he strode across the room and pulled Simone to her feet. Wrapping his arms around her waist, he lowered his head toward her and kissed her softly on the lips.

"What was that for?" she asked when he finally broke off the kiss.

"For being the best wife a man could ask for." Marcus cupped her face in his hands and brushed his fingers tenderly across her cheeks. Seeing how much she'd enjoyed the attention from his friends bothered him. No, it hurt. Simone didn't hop on anybody's lap or shake her butt in anybody's face, but she beamed and giggled whenever someone paid her a compliment. Marcus didn't need to look inside her head to know she was feeling unloved and neglected, but from now on he'd make sure his wife knew how much he cared for her.

"I love you, Simone. I know I don't always tell you or show you how I feel, but I do," he whispered, meaning every word. "Sorry for not being here for you, like you need me to be, but from now on I promise to be a better husband and father."

Her eyes lit up and sparkled with excitement. "That means a lot to me to hear you say that."

"Maybe we can do something together on Saturday."

"Sorry, baby, but I already have plans."

Marcus raised an eyebrow. "You do?"

"Yeah, I'm taking the boys to a birthday party in the afternoon, and in the evening the girls and I are doing dinner and a movie," she explained. "I can't wait to see the new Tyler Perry movie. It's gotten great reviews, and it was number one at the box office last week."

"I thought we were going to see it together. You know I love his movies."

Frowning, she slanted her head to the right. "I asked you

if you wanted to see it, but you said you didn't have time, remember?"

Marcus scratched his head. He didn't remember saying that, but if he was checking his email on his cell phone or working in his office at the time, he'd probably missed the question and mumbled a response. Hence, why he had no recollection of the conversation now.

"Why don't you come with us to the birthday party? It would be nice if you finally met Jayden and Jordan's friends and some of the other parents."

"But I want to spend time with you, *alone,*" he argued, lowering his mouth to her neck and playfully nipping at her earlobe. "Ever since you started at Friendship House we hardly see each other. Sometimes it feels like we're two ships passing in the night."

Simone laughed. "Baby, quit being so dramatic. We made love a couple days ago."

Marcus felt like he'd been kicked in the stomach. Dropping his hands from around her waist, he slumped back against the leather couch. "Is that what you think? That the only reason I want to spend time with you is so we can have sex?"

"I don't know. Isn't it?"

He was so stunned by her words, so bewildered, he couldn't speak.

"I'm beat," Simone said, patting back a yawn. "I'm going up to bed."

Marcus swallowed the lump in his throat and forced a smile. "I'll be up in a minute. Thanks again for tonight, baby. The food was delicious, and my friends had a great time."

"I love hosting parties, but your friends wore me out with their incessant chatter. They're worse than Jayden and Jordan, and those two talk nonstop!"

Marcus watched his wife slowly climb the spiral staircase. Long after Simone left and disappeared into the master bedroom, he sat slumped against the couch, thinking about what she'd said. Feelings of sadness engulfed him, and it didn't matter how many times he told himself Simone loved him and was committed to their marriage, he still felt a suffocating ache in his chest. He felt alone, empty inside, like a man who'd lost his one true love. And the worst thing about it was, Marcus didn't know what to do about it.

Chapter 15

A dramatic cold front brought snow, ice and golf-ball-size hail to the Windy City the first week in November. And when Simone woke up on Monday morning and heard the wind whacking tree branches against her window, she considered staying in bed until the storm blew over. The room was drenched in darkness, but she heard the familiar chug of city snowplows, shovels scraping against sidewalks and the buzz of rush-hour traffic.

Simone swallowed a yawn. Marcus had his arms wrapped around her, and his scent was so clean, so refreshing, she felt a deep sense of peace. He stirred, tightened his grip on her waist. These were the moments Simone loved, the moments that were ingrained in her heart and mind. When Marcus cradled her to his chest she felt safe, secure, and although things had been tense between them ever since she had started her new job last month, Simone wouldn't trade this quiet, intimate time for anything in the world.

Last night, she'd had his favorite meal waiting for him

when he'd returned home early from work. After putting the boys to bed, Simone slipped into an itty-bitty negligee and sauntered into the living room with a saucy smile on her lips and a bottle of Shiraz in her hands. Their lovemaking had always been passionate, but last night was arms-flailing, heart-throbbing, toe-curling good.

Simone didn't know if the sex was better because of her newfound self-confidence or because she'd taken her mother-in-law's advice and quit nagging him, but their lovemaking was sizzling. And after the third dizzying round, the living room lamp lay in pieces on the carpet and cushion stuffing was floating in the air like snow drifting down from the sky.

Welcoming the memories, she felt a smile explode over her face. Urgent kisses, urgent hands, urgent strokes. The soft, angelic voice of R & B singer Faith Evans ushering them into a lover's paradise. A light breeze gliding through the window. A star-rich sky christening the living room with its tender light.

That's why Simone wanted to play hooky from work today. She wanted to spend the day with Marcus, in bed, doing nothing but talking and cuddling and making love. Isn't that what life was all about? Doing things that made you happy. That's what Jaxson Stafford preached during their weekly sessions. Ever since Simone started meeting with the famed attorney slash therapist, she felt more relaxed and less stressed out.

One afternoon a week, inside his chic downtown office, Simone unburdened her heart. They discussed her marriage, the kids, the pain of not knowing who her father was. Jaxson Stafford asked poignant questions, ones designed for soul-searching, and every week Simone left his office with no intention of returning. But she did. And arrived early, too! They had an appointment scheduled for Wednesday morning, and Simone was going to ask Marcus to join her. It was time they worked together to improve their marriage, and she had a feeling her husband and the charismatic attorney would hit it off.

Simone glanced at the alarm clock. Still plenty of time to luxuriate in bed. In an hour, she'd get up and make breakfast, and over coffee she'd tell Marcus how much she was enjoying her sessions with Jaxson Stafford. Then, they'd drop the boys off at school and spend the rest of the day hanging out in the city. But when Simone remembered that she had three home visits scheduled for that afternoon, and mountains of paperwork on her desk, she slipped from between the covers and left the comfort of her husband's warm arms.

Cursing Old Man Winter, Simone dragged her sleep-deprived body out of bed just as dawn was breaking over the horizon. Careful not to wake Marcus, she showered, dressed in her favorite Chanel business suit and packed her briefcase. Slipping out of the room with the stealth of a cat burglar, she closed the door and tiptoed down the darkened hallway.

A quick check in on the boys, a cup of cappuccino and Simone was ready to face the day. And those treacherous Chicago streets. The drive across town was a long, nerve-racking journey, but when Simone pulled into the Friendship House parking lot and saw that no one else was there, a frown burned her lips. The streets were bad, but not *that* bad.

Simone shouldn't have been surprised. Friendship House was the busiest nonprofit center in the city, but it was badly understaffed and the employee turnover rate was ridiculously high. Employees called in sick on a weekly basis and often quit at a moment's notice. Most of the veteran staff members were biding their time until they got a "real job" in the cushy, downtown office overlooking Millennium Park. Well, everyone expect Simone. She loved the inner city, loved the strength and courage of its residents, and couldn't imagine working anywhere else.

After unlocking the door and disabling the alarm, she flipped on the lights and opened the cranberry-colored blinds. The exterior of the building was in need of an extreme makeover, but the reception area was a wide, colorful space filled with green leafy plants, vibrant artwork and padded armchairs.

Simone put on coffee, jacked up the thermostat as high as

it would go and strode to the back of the building. Inside her cramped but functional office, Simone sat down at her desk and turned on the computer. Before she could type in her password, the telephone rang. *It's probably someone calling in sick,* she thought, pressing line one. "Hello, Friendship House."

"Is, ah, Mr. Gladstone there?"

"I'm sorry. He's not in. Would you care to leave a message?"

After a lengthy pause, the woman blurted out, "My son is missing."

Before Simone could advise the caller to phone the authorities, the woman broke into tears. Cried so loud Simone had to move the phone away from her ear. "Ma'am, you—"

"He's been missing since Friday," she said, between deep, racking sobs, "and if I call the police they'll take him away from me. I need my boy here to help me take care of his younger sisters." The woman sniffled, coughed like she had a bad cold. "He's seventeen and for the most part a good kid, but ever since my husband died last year…"

Filled with compassion, Simone listened quietly as the caller spoke fondly about her teenage son. Making brief notes on her notepad, she prayed that Mr. Gladstone would arrive soon and help this distraught mother find her missing son.

"A neighbor spotted him at Rupert's Café. Said he was smoking and everything. I wanted to go down there to look for him, but I didn't have anyone to leave my other kids with."

Simone raised an eyebrow and gripped the receiver tighter. *What's a seventeen-year-old boy doing at Rupert's Café?* Rupert's, as the locals called it, was a popular hangout spot for drug dealers, con artists, hoodlums and the like. "Ma'am, is your son in a gang?"

"No. Never." Despite her anguish, her tone was strong, resolute. "Things have been tough ever since my Charlie died, but I'm doing the best I can for me and my kids."

Her words touched Simone deeply. She was a mother, too;

she understood. Simone didn't make it a habit to enter gang territory, and she knew Marcus would kill her if he ever found out she went to Rupert's Cafe, but she couldn't sit around and do nothing. "What's your son's name?"

"Lester, but everyone calls him—"

"Hoops," Simone finished, lowering her ballpoint pen. Everyone in the neighborhood knew who Lester "Hoops" DeWitt was. And not just because he stood head and shoulders above his peers. Dubbed "Hoops" after he had shattered every basketball record in the state, Lester had not only led his team to the state championships last year, but also brought back the first-place trophy. "Ms. DeWitt, I'm not going to make any promises, but—"

"You're going to go out and look for Lester? You're going to bring my baby home?" Her voice rose hysterically. "Thank you! Thank you so much!"

Simone took down Ms. DeWitt's phone number and promised to have someone call her within the hour. Clipping her badge on her jacket, she walked out of her office and into the now-bustling reception area. Bonita Guerrero, the perky secretary who had aspirations of being a reality TV star, was sitting behind her desk, trolling online gossip sites.

"Is Isaiah in?" Simone asked.

"No, not yet. He's visiting a family on the Lower East Side."

"Any idea how long he'll be?"

"Shouldn't be too long, why?"

Simone told Bonita about her conversation with Mrs. DeWitt, then handed over her contact notes. "Do you mind phoning Isaiah and letting him know what's going on? Since he's already on the South Side, he can go speak to Mrs. DeWitt in person and then look for Hoops."

"No problem, Mrs. Young. I'll get right on it!"

The rest of the morning was long and uneventful, and by the time eleven o'clock rolled around, Simone was ready for a break. She'd spent the past four hours chained to her desk, filing out reports and filling paperwork. Meeting with the clients on her caseload and finding solutions to their problems was the highlight of her day. Doing paperwork was not. That's why Simone had the radio on, the blinds drawn and a large bowl of chocolate almonds at her fingertips.

Simone needed a pick-me-up, someone to make her laugh, and she thought of Marcus. As she reached for the phone to dial his private number, it rang. "Hello. Simone Young speaking."

"Why, hello, Simone Young. This is your drop-dead gorgeous husband, Marcus Young. How are you doing this morning, beautiful?"

A smile overwhelmed Simone's mouth. "You're crazy."

"Only about you."

"Well, aren't we full of compliments and sweet words today?" she joked, leaning back and resting comfortably in her chair. "You have great timing. I was just about to call you."

"I would hope so. What's up with sneaking off this morning without giving me some loving? You know doing you is my favorite way to start off my day."

"You looked so tired this morning, I didn't want to wake you."

"Excuses, excuses," he scoffed, chuckling. "I'm going to make you pay tonight!"

"I look forward to it...."

"Awww, sookie, sookie, now!"

The couple shared a laugh.

"Are you still coming with me to the mayor's luncheon on the twenty-ninth?"

"Of course. Why wouldn't I?"

"I was just checking," he explained after a brief pause. "You just started your new job and I didn't think you'd want to take time off so soon."

"We go every year, and I enjoy meeting all your friends and business associates."

"Cool. I was hoping you'd say that!"

Simone heard the smile in her husband's voice, knew that

he was wearing the biggest, widest grin. "How's your day going?"

"Rough. I'm down to one towel boy, and the men's changing room looks like a pigsty. Hey, how do you feel about me hiring Jayden and Jordan part-time?"

Imagining the boys scurrying around Samson's Gym, picking up after burly muscle men in spandex, made Simone laugh. Thinking about her kids reminded Simone of her early-morning conversation with Mrs. DeWitt, the widowed mother looking for her teenage son. An idea sparked in her mind, one that made her so excited, she shot up in her chair. "Hey, I know someone you can hire! He's a star athlete who could use a strong male influence in his life. You know, someone smart and successful and intelligent like you."

"God, I love when you stroke my ego."

"Just your ego?"

"Baby, don't start something you can't finish."

"Okay, I'll save the explicit talk for the bedroom."

"Good idea." His voice turned serious. "What's the name of the kid you want me to hire?"

"Lester DeWitt."

"The high school basketball star?"

"Yeah, that's him. He lost his dad last year in a tragic car accident and has been running around with the wrong crowd ever since."

"Poor kid. That's terrible. I'll talk to Nate, but I'm sure we can find something better for him to do than just collect towels. He's one hell of an athlete, and from what I've read about him, he's smart, too."

"Thanks, baby. You're the best!"

"I know, that's what I keep telling you!"

Simone giggled.

"Let's watch a movie later, just you and me."

"No," she quipped, rolling her eyes, "you mean me, you and your beloved cell phone."

"Nope, I'm going to leave it in the bedroom."

"Better yet, don't even bring it into the house!"

Marcus chuckled, a deep, rumbling laugh. "Put the boys to bed early tonight and meet me at the door in those black stilettos I bought you in Manchester," he ordered, in a smooth, take-charge tone. "I can't wait to have you, baby. Been thinking about it all day, kissing you, tasting you, thrusting myself so deep inside you that you scream my name."

A shudder passed through her, caused her temperature to soar like a rocket. His words sent waves of desire through her, aroused her, made her feel so sexy she could hardly handle it. Under her blouse, her nipples hardened, grew so sensitive, Simone felt the urge to touch herself. Only Marcus could do this to her. She wished he was there, in her office, making good on his promises.

"I'm going to do you on the staircase, the washing machine, and the—"

"Baby, that's risky. You know Jordan is a light sleeper."

"Are you turning me down?"

"Never," she purred, coiling the phone cord around her index finger. "I just don't want one of the boys catching us in the act and telling our family and friends about the encounter!"

"I don't know if I can wait until tonight," he rasped, his voice a throaty whisper. "Maybe I should swing by your office for a little visit."

Simone shook her head, giggled like a tween when he promised to make it the most memorable lunch break of her life. "Are you trying to get me fired?"

"No, I'm trying to make you come…."

"Ummm…" she breathed, wishing they were home, in bed, making sweet love on their soft, satin sheets. After making love, they'd talk and cuddle and discuss their day. She always loved that time. Loved when it was just the two of them, alone, sharing their deepest feelings and thoughts. Simone stared at the clock, calculated the hours until she'd see her husband again. *I was thinking of taking Jayden and Jordan to Pizzapoplis tonight but some things are more important than eating overpriced pizza and playing video games,* she decided, a smirk tickling her lips. *Like spending quality time with my busy husband.*

"Oh, snap!"

Simone shook free of her thoughts. "What's wrong?"

"The Bodybuilding and Fitness Championships starts tonight, and I'm on the judging panel," he explained. "A reminder just popped up on my phone."

Disappointment filled her, stealing her smile and the joy she'd felt only seconds earlier. She wanted to beg Marcus to cancel, to just come home and spend the night with her, but she rejected the thought. She had to stop using Marcus to fill the void in her life left by her father and basing her happiness on what he did or didn't do.

"Sorry, baby, but I'll have to take a rain check on movie night."

"That's fine," she lied, wishing it was. "I'm tired anyways. I probably would've fallen asleep during the previews!"

"So, you're not mad?"

"Why would I be mad? You have to work. That's life."

Marcus stared down at the phone receiver, his eyes wide with wonder. *Did Simone just say what I* think *she said?* These days, nothing seemed to faze her. She was more patient with Jayden and Jordan, didn't trip when he had to work late and was even getting along better with his mom. That, in and of itself, was a miracle.

"I'm going to make this up to you, baby, you'll see."

"That's what you keep telling me."

"I'm for real this time," he insisted. "I'll clear my schedule for next Saturday and we'll spend all day in bed. It'll be like we were back in Manchester, except without the butler!"

"Will Angela be planning it, too?" Simone blurted. The second the words left her mouth, she wished she could reel them back in. It was hard, but she had to stop throwing Marcus's mistakes back in his face. That's something she'd learned from the little pink book, and Gladys, and for the last few weeks she'd made a concerted effort not to argue with him about every small, trivial thing. From now on she wasn't going to depend on Marcus for her happiness, or expect him to be a perfect husband or father. She was going to concentrate on all the great things in her life and quit stressing about the problems in her marriage.

An awkward silence settled over the line, and when Marcus finally spoke, she could hear the sadness in his tone, and that made her feel petty and immature.

"I didn't ask Angela to help me because I was being lazy, Simone. I just wanted everything to be perfect for you."

"I know." Simone felt her eyes tear up, and she cleared her throat. "I better go. I have tons of paperwork to do, and you have that bodybuilding thing."

"Thanks for being so understanding, baby."

"Have fun tonight, Marcus. I'll see you later!"

Marcus didn't realize she'd hung up the phone until he heard the dial tone buzzing in his ear. Dumbfounded, he stared down at the phone receiver. Simone sounded happy, excited even, but Marcus had a feeling he'd just bought himself a one-way ticket to the couch.

Chapter 16

"I won!" Marcus shouted, raising his hands in triumph as he powered past the finish line of Samson's four-hundred-meter indoor track. "I told you I could still whoop your ass in a race!"

Doubled over, his hands propped on his knees, L. J. Saunders huffed and puffed like the Little Engine that Could. He was panting so loudly, the muscle men in the weight area were pointing and laughing. "I—I just need a minute to catch my breath."

After a prolonged moment of silence, L.J. straightened his bent shoulders and stood to his full height. "I want a rematch."

"Forget it. I beat you fair and square!"

"Sure you did," he scoffed, wiping the sweat spilling down his bald head with the bottom of his T-shirt. "You cutting me off at that last corner had absolutely nothing to do with it."

Marcus clapped his friend on the shoulder. "Let's go grab a drink, because you look like you're about to kick the bucket, and I don't want your wife to kill me!"

Located across the street from Samson's Gym, Della's Joint

was the place to go for finger-lickin'-good down-home cooking. The food at the family-owned restaurant was outstanding, the waiters were friendly and the simple decor was rich in color. Marcus and L.J. sat on round swivel stools facing the front window, eating out of wicker baskets filled with ribs, sweet potato fries and cornbread. It was Friday evening, around the time the dinner rush usually started, but aside from the trio of bikers playing pool, and the teenage couple squabbling a few tables over, the restaurant was quiet.

"I wasn't kidding about that rematch," L.J. said, pointing his fork at his longtime friend. "If I wasn't flying out later tonight, I'd race you first thing tomorrow morning."

"Living in D.C. has made you soft. Quit whining and toughen up."

"Taking that position with the Wizards turned out to be the best decision I've ever made." Pride filled his eyes and his tone. "Next to marrying Autumn, of course."

Marcus licked the barbecue sauce off his fingers. "You sound like a typical newlywed. Head over heels in love and willing to move heaven and earth to make your woman happy."

"We're hardly newlyweds. We got married before you and Simone did, remember?"

Nodding, Marcus raised the oversize mason jar to his lips and took a long swig of his root beer. "So, how are you guys doing? Thinking about starting a family yet?"

"I'm working on it, man, and having a helluva time trying, too!"

His laughter bounced off the walls, lightened the mood in the air.

"We're having so much fun traveling and enjoying being a twosome that we haven't given parenthood much thought."

"I'm not surprised. Every time I talk to you you're jetting off somewhere."

"I know, cool, huh?" L.J. looked proud, like a golfer who'd struck a hole in one.

Marcus glanced at his watch. "We better hurry up or we're going to miss the fight."

"I'm not going to Champions tonight."

"Why not? The Bishop-Lipenski rematch is the most anticipated match of the year!"

"I'm taking Autumn out on a date."

"Can't you wine and dine her tomorrow?"

"I can, but I don't want to," he answered, leaning back in his seat. "Rashawn 'The Glove' Bishop is one bad dude in the ring, but I'd rather hang out with my wife."

Marcus closed his mouth before it hit the table. He couldn't believe that L.J., an executive for the Washington Wizards who watched every sporting event known to man, was going to miss the biggest fight of the year. "So, what are you two doing this weekend?"

"You mean besides each other?" L.J. wore a sly grin. "Autumn's addicted to that reality show *So You Think You Can Cook,* so I booked the chef for a private cooking lesson."

"Why go to a class when you can just cook at home?"

"Because I want my woman to feel special."

Marcus didn't know why, but listening to L.J. gush about his wife made him feel low, guilty, like the day he'd foolishly left his wife in Manchester. "I wish I could take Simone out every weekend, too, but my new business ventures are eating up all of my free time."

"I don't have that problem anymore. When I get home from work, I turn off my cell and drop it in my briefcase. No excuses. No exceptions."

"My staff would have a heart attack if I ever did that."

"Trust me, they'll survive." L.J. popped a fry into his mouth and chewed furiously. "I was engaged briefly back in the day, and that chick dogged me out so bad, I thought I'd never recover. Then I met Autumn. She means everything to me, so I put her first. Period."

"Don't start crying." Marcus wore a stern voice, but his

tone was alive with humor. "If you do, I'll never be able to show my face in here again!"

The men chuckled, bumped elbows in jest.

"Take it from someone who's been happily married for years. The secret to a successful marriage is making time to connect with your spouse every day."

Marcus raised an eyebrow. "That's it?"

"That's it. And do all the little things you did in the beginning to catch her eye. Serve her breakfast in bed, shower her with compliments, post love notes on the bathroom mirror..."

Marcus wished he had a pen so he could take notes. What L.J. said made perfect sense and didn't cost a thing, but where was he going to find the time to romance his wife? He had to prep for his meeting with the Chicago Bears, write another article for *Bodybuilders Magazine* and hold a second round of interviews for the assistant manager position.

"You know what my aunt Ruthie told me on my wedding day?"

"I don't have the faintest idea," Marcus teased, assuming a Southern accent. "Do tell."

"She said, 'Love your wife like you've known her for years, but romance her like you've known her for days.'"

"Wow, that's deep."

"I know, huh?"

"Loving Simone is easy—it's finding time to do the romance stuff that's hard as hell."

"You're like me, a classic type A perfectionist who gets so caught up in your work you lose sight of what's important in life. But to have a healthy marriage you have make your spouse a priority." L.J. raised his jar and tipped it in his friend's direction. "The challenge is to find balance. A happy medium that you and your wife can live with."

"I wasn't always this way, but my business took off at warp speed, and—"

L.J. cut him off. "Man, please. You've been like this since college. Driven, intense, ridiculously focused. You managed the hell out of that burger joint near campus, and, as I recall, you were named employee of the month like five times in one year!"

"It was nine, but who's counting?"

The men chuckled. The conversation turned to sports, then a heated discussion about politics. Time flew by. The sun faded, leaving the sky a maelstrom of deep blues and somber grays. The clouds looked like thick puffs of smoke and seemed to stretch from one end of the heavens to the next. A distinct chill filled the restaurant, and the scent of apple pie sweetened the air.

"Oh, there goes my phone." Marcus pulled out his cell and read his newest text message. "I better run. It's going to take me about an hour to drive across town, and Nate said the last one at Champions has to pick up the tab!"

"You're still going to watch the fight?"

"I might as well. I have nothing else going on tonight."

"Maybe instead of going to Champions, you should go home and plan a romantic evening for your wife," he proposed. "After a long, tiring day at the office that's exactly what she needs, *and* if you go all out tonight, you'll be in her good books for weeks to come."

Marcus gave it some thought. These days, Simone was spending more time away from home, which meant less time with him. If she wasn't at Friendship House or driving around the city collecting donations on behalf of her clients, she was hanging out at Angela's house or taking the boys someplace or the other. He couldn't remember the last time they'd went out, and it had been weeks since they'd had an honest, open talk. Ever since the whole bodybuilding tournament fiasco he hadn't been able to get close to her. *That's all the more reason to go home.*

Stroking his jaw, he considered the advice L.J. had given him. Maybe on the way home, he'd stop at Discreet Boutiques and have a quick look around. He thought about their trip to Manchester, smiled when he remembered how much fun they'd had making out in one of the lingerie fitting rooms. But what stuck out most in his mind was the time they'd spent talking and cuddling in bed. He loved that he could open up to Simone, loved that he could share his feelings and thoughts freely with her.

Marcus felt a jolt of adrenaline, of excitement. He didn't know if it was the thought of surprising Simone that thrilled him or spending the rest of the night holding the woman he loved in his arms, but he couldn't wait to execute his plan. Tonight wasn't about sex. It was about reconnecting with Simone, about showing her how much he cared and adored her. That's why instead of going to Discreet Boutiques to buy his wife lingerie, he was going to stop by her favorite florist shop and buy Simone the biggest, most lavish flower bouquet she'd ever seen.

"You know what, L.J.?" Marcus said, tossing down his napkin and jumping to his feet. "You're a sore loser, and so badly out of shape my five-year-old sons could beat you in a race, but that's the smartest thing you've said all night!"

Chapter 17

"Open up, already," Simone grumbled, jabbing the buzzer of her mother-in-law's brown brick home for the third time. It was freezing, well below the thirty degrees forecasters had predicted, and Simone feared if Gladys didn't open up soon, she'd have frostbite from ear to toe.

What is she doing? Simone wondered, rubbing her gloved hands together. She could hear the TV blaring and blasts of raucous laughter, and every light in the house was on. Simone considered calling Gladys, but that would require returning to the car for her cell phone, and she was feeling lazy. *And* cold.

Banging on the kitchen window, like a member of the police S.W.A.T. team, produced immediate results. The door creaked open, one ridiculously slow inch at a time, and when Simone saw her brother-in-law standing against the frame, in a black tank top, skull cap and gray sweats hanging precariously off his waist, she swallowed a groan. He had a beer bottle in one hand and the remote control in the other.

"Hey, Derek," she said, stepping inside the foyer and shutting the door behind her. "Can you let the boys know that I'm here?"

"Mom took the boys grocery shopping with her," he explained, his worlds slightly slurred. "They went to that new place on Ninth."

On any other day, Simone would have walked over to the supermarket to meet the boys and do some grocery shopping of her own, but after meeting Angela for lunch and eating three slices of deep-dish pizza, she felt like an overstuffed piñata. All she wanted to do was pick up Jayden and Jordan and go home. "Any idea when they'll be back?"

"Shouldn't be long. Come inside and chill for a minute."

Pretending not to hear his suggestion, she asked if Gladys had her cell phone with her. Her mother-in-law routinely forgot her phone at home and would tell anyone who listened that cell phones were corrupting today's youth, one salacious text message at a time.

"Yeah, she has it on her. Hang tight. I'll go hit her up."

"Don't worry. I'll phone her from the car." Simone unlocked the screen door, buried her face in her wool jacket and prepared to face the bitter cold. "Bye, Derek, have a good night."

"Hey, hold up! Do you have a fifty I can hold until payday?"

Simone shook her head. Even if she had it, she wouldn't have given it to Derek, but since she was making a concerted effort to be nicer to her brother-in-law, she spoke in her softest, kindest voice. "Sorry, I wish I did, but I don't."

"Sure you don't." He rasped a laugh. "I bet you have all kinds of money now that you up and found yourself a job. My brother doesn't make enough for you, huh, college girl?"

Simone glared at him. "Some people prefer to *work,* instead of lying around all day watching TV and drinking beer."

"Have you always been this stuck-up, or did your head swell after you sunk your claws into my kid brother?"

"Excuse me?"

"You heard me," he snapped, raising the beer bottle to his

lips and gulping some down. "You think you're better than me because you have a degree, but you're not. You got lucky. Remember that. You. Got. Lucky."

"Luck had nothing to do with it. I worked two minimum-wage jobs to put myself through school, and busted my butt to graduate with honors."

"Don't front, college girl. The only reason you're pushing a Benz and living in that expensive community up in the boondocks is because you married my brother."

"Are you high?" Simone winced when she heard the question tumble out of her mouth, but she didn't apologize. Derek was talking crazy, and she wasn't going to put up with his mess. Not after the long, stressful afternoon she'd had at Friendship House. "I'm out of here."

Unlocking the screen door, she pushed it open and stomped back down the steps. Snow blew into her face, and the wind whipped her hair around, lashing her cheeks and neck.

"You should be thanking your lucky stars that Marcus is a responsible, stand-up guy," Derek continued. "Because if you had showed up at my house sobbing hysterically about being pregnant I would have slammed the door in your face."

Simone wheeled around and stared down the belligerent fool. She imagined wrestling that beer bottle out of Derek's hand and whacking him in the head with it. Was he out of his mind? How dare he speak to her like that! He wouldn't dream of insulting her if Marcus or Gladys was around, but because they were alone he was freely running his mouth.

"Face it, toots," he jeered. "My brother only married you because you got knocked up."

"That's not true."

"Yeah, it is. You threatened to put his babies up for adoption, so he popped the question."

Shame filled Simone. "Is that what Marcus told you?"

"Don't worry about it, college girl. You just go on living in your perfect world, and looking down on everybody else. I'm going to make something of myself—" he jabbed a finger at his chest "—and it won't be because I rode somebody's coattails, either. I'm…"

Tears blinded her eyes, made it impossible for Simone to see, but she fled the house and rushed down the snow-covered walkway. She wasn't going to give Derek the satisfaction of seeing her cry. He was lying, making up stories to hurt her, trying to ruin her already bad day. But if all that was true, how did he know that she'd shown up on Marcus's doorstep the night she had learned she was pregnant? And sobbing, no less?

Simone refused to cry, she just wasn't going to do it, wasn't going to dissolve into tears like she had that afternoon her doctor confirmed that she was pregnant with twins. But once Simone slid into the front seat of her car and sped off down the block, far away from Derek and his cruel, baseless accusations, the tears fell so fast and furious, she had to pull over.

Sprinkle or toss? Marcus stared down at the package of rose petals in his hands, unsure of what to do with it. *How come it doesn't come with directions*? He thought of calling L.J., but knew he'd lose major cool points with the fellas if word ever got out. Marcus could hear them laughing now, see them pointing and pelting him in the face with beer nuts.

Deciding it didn't matter, he scattered large handfuls across the bedroom floor, making a trail from the door to the candlelit table he'd set with china and around the bed. "Shoot, I forget to grab the wine," he said, noticing the empty, ice-filled bucket. Once the package of red rose petals was empty and the master bedroom looked exotic, Marcus headed downstairs.

On the bottom shelf in kitchen pantry, he perused the rows of vintage bottles. He hated creamy flavors that tasted sweeter than ice cream, but he selected the brand that Simone liked. Had to. Two glasses of it, and his wife became more amorous than the character in *She's Gotta Have It*. And tonight, he had to have *her*.

As Marcus stood, he spotted a glossy, white business card at his feet. The word *home* was scrawled on it, and underneath was a local area number. Tucking the wine bottle under his arm, he picked up the card and flipped it over. When he saw the name on the card, in large, bold, block letters, his skin paled five shades.

Scared he was going to drop the wine bottle, he placed it on the counter and tried to calm himself down. Staring intently at the card, Marcus searched it for clues. What was Jaxson Stafford's business card doing in his house? And why was his home number written on the back? Marcus had never met the famed divorce attorney, but he sure as hell knew who he was. Everyone did. Hailed as the Johnny Cochran of the East Coast, the thirty-year-old Chicago native had a reputation for bedding his clients—married and otherwise—and after Angela featured him on her "Young, Rich and Powerful" segment his popularity had shot through the roof.

There was a logical explanation for this, Marcus told himself. Had to be. Simone must have called Jaxson on behalf of one of her clients. *Right, that's it,* his inner voice jeered. *She's counseling an über-rich woman who can afford the hotshot attorney's six-figure retainer!*

Marcus coughed. Unless *Simone* was the über-rich woman seeking Mr. Stafford's services. His throat burned, stung so bad he couldn't swallow. It could only mean one thing: Simone wanted a…a… He stumbled over the word, couldn't bring himself to say it. He crumpled the business card and chucked it on the floor.

He couldn't believe it, couldn't wrap his head around the truth. Simone had hired an attorney, and not just any attorney, but a man who had an impeccable track record. A man with a reputation for slicing and dicing his opponents in open court.

His hands curled into fists. Marcus wanted to punch something—hard, wanted to find an outlet for his anger, but he wouldn't trash his home, the place where his kids lived and played. His sons.

Jayden and Jordan were his universe, the reason why he

pushed himself to accomplish every dream, every goal. Simone knew that. So why would she do something like this?

Hanging his head, he ran his hands down the length of his face. He was…was… Marcus couldn't find the words, couldn't identify what he was feeling inside. He was upset, angry, sure, but he was hurt more than anything. Things had been strained ever since he opened his sixth Samson's Gym location, and now with Simone working he hardly saw her anymore, but that didn't mean he was ready to throw in the towel. He wasn't. Not ever. On their wedding day, he'd vowed to God and that jovial minister who kept cracking jokes that he'd love and protect Simone until the day he died. She'd made the same vow, the same promise. Had it all been a lie? Something she said, but didn't truly mean—

"You're home."

He'd been so caught up in his thoughts, he didn't hear Simone come in. Marcus turned to face her and wished to God he hadn't. Her beauty had an incandescent quality to it, a truly striking glow that stole his breath every time. He admired her creamy brown skin, her delicious, pouty lips, the seductive curve of her hips outlined in her black, fitted suit. She looked good to him. *Real good.* Always had, always would. He wanted to welcome her home with a hug and a kiss, like they usually did at the end of a long day, but then he remembered she was sneaking around with Jaxson Stafford and plunged his hands into his jeans pocket.

"I thought you were going to the bar to watch boxing with your friends."

His mouth was dry, but he managed to speak. "I changed my mind."

Simone dumped her briefcase at her feet. Papers spilled out, landing in a heap on the floor, but she didn't pick them up. She didn't have the energy. Not tonight. For the past hour, she'd driven around aimlessly, replaying her argument with Derek and trying to figure out why Marcus would tell his brother about the lowest moment in her life. Simone didn't want to talk to him, and if she'd known Marcus was home she would have gone to Angela's house. *Or not,* she thought, recalling her conversation with her best friend earlier in the day. Angela was en route to Philadelphia to chase down another hot lead for her "Athletes Behaving Badly" exposé. A scowl bruised Simone's lips. *They're not the only ones behaving badly.*

"Where are the boys?" Marcus asked, his tone thin, flat.

"I went to pick them up from your mom's, but Derek said they went grocery shopping. I called Gladys, and she promised to drop them off soon."

"God, I hate when you do that."

"Do what?"

"Say my brother's name with such disgust."

Her eyes filled with wide-eyed innocence. "I don't like men who abuse women," she said tightly. "I'm sorry if that bothers you, but guys like Derek make me sick."

"He paid his debt to society, Simone, but since you brought up the assault case, might I remind you that his ex-girlfriend hit him first. She admitted as much in court."

"Yeah, probably because Derek threatened her with bodily harm."

My brother's not perfect, and he's messed up a lot over the years, but at least he's loyal—"

Simone broke in. "At least *someone* in your family is."

"What's that supposed to mean?"

"Why did you tell Derek about that night?"

"What night?"

"The night I told you I was pregnant."

Marcus hung his head. *Damn.* What had his brother done now?

"After calling me a gold digger, Derek repeated everything I said to you verbatim!" she yelled, venting her anger. "How could you, Marcus? How could you share my deepest, darkest feelings with someone who'd one day throw it back in my face?"

Shame singed his cheeks, spread like fire down his neck.

Marcus remembered that blistering summer night with astounding clarity. Still, even after all these years. He'd opened his front door, and Simone had literally fallen into his arms—crying, shaking, on the brink of hysteria. To comfort her, he'd cradled her to his chest and led her inside. Once her tears had subsided, she'd told him everything. About how a blood test at her doctor's office revealed that she was pregnant, and that the ultrasound confirmed she was carrying twins. It was like someone had sucked all the air out of the room. His entire body had gone numb. He couldn't breathe, couldn't think, and his head had pounded so violently he'd feared he was having a stroke.

"I can't believe you'd tell Derek something you know I'm ashamed of. Do you have any idea how hard it was for me to come to your place that night?"

"I needed someone to talk to," he admitted, shaking off the memories of her heart-wrenching confession, "so I turned to Derek for some brotherly advice."

"You could have confided in anyone, but instead of choosing someone mature and wise you told my business to Derek. *Real* fine choice, Marcus."

"I'm not going to apologize for confiding in my brother."

Simone fired back, "Good. Don't. I didn't ask you to."

"Whatever. It's in the past. Let it go."

"You know what, Marcus? Sometimes you can be a real jerk."

"I know." He barked a bitter laugh. "That's what you keep telling me."

"God, I'm so sick of fighting with you! You don't appreciate me, or all the things I do to make you happy. All you do is take, take, take—"

"Is that why you hired Jaxson Stafford? Because you want out of this marriage?"

Simone paused, sucked in a deep breath. Not because she needed time to prepare an answer, but because the question stunned her.

"So it's true. You've been meeting with that clown behind my back."

"It's not like that."

"Oh, no, what's it like?"

"He's not just an attorney. He's a licensed therapist, who I've been seeing for the past month—" Simone paused when she saw her husband wince. His face was red, and the veins in his neck were stretched so tight his eyes were twitching. "I was apprehensive about going to counseling at first, but talking to someone about how I'm feeling really helps."

"I bet it does. Apparently, he has a way with words that drive women wild."

Simone ignored the jab and continued speaking. "I have an appointment scheduled for tomorrow, and I'd like you to come. I think talking to a professional will help us work through some of our issues."

"Cancel the appointment, Simone. I'm not going, and neither are you."

"Excuse me?"

"You heard me."

"You can't tell me what to do, Marcus. I'm your wife, not a piece of property," she shot back, refusing to wither under his piercing gaze. "Jaxson's an incredible therapist, and—"

"Oh, so you guys are on a first-name basis? How professional."

"We are now that he's agreed to do some pro bono work for Friendship House."

"You're going to be working with that clown, too?"

"What's the matter with you? Why are you getting so upset?"

Marcus shouted his words. "Because he's a divorce attorney, Simone! A divorce attorney who screws his clients, then brags about it to his friends! His colleagues work out at Samson's and you should hear the way they talk. They're raunchy and lewd...."

Simone felt like screaming, like releasing all of the day's

frustration in one loud, ear-piercing wail. First, she'd argued with Mr. Gladstone about how he'd botched the Lester De-Witt case, then Derek verbally attacked her and now Marcus was accusing her of having an inappropriate relationship with her therapist. Simone scoffed, rolled her eyes at the ludicrous claim. As if she'd ever cheat on Marcus. Didn't he know how much she loved him, how thankful she was to have him in her life?

"There's nothing going on between me and Jaxson. I talk and he listens. That's it."

"Have you ever discussed ending our marriage with him?"

Her first inclination was to lie, to say something mean and cruel that would hurt him, the way his betrayal had hurt her, but she didn't, couldn't. "No. Never."

"Sure," he said, folding his arms. "You're lying. You can't even look me in the eye."

That's because my heart can't take any more pain! Simone willed herself not to cry, not to break down like she had that night in Marcus's living room. "Why does it matter? It's not like you love me. You only married me because I got pregnant, remember?"

Marcus slammed the pantry door so hard, the glasses in the cabinet shook. He stared at her for a long, intense moment, then dropped his hands to his sides. "I'm done."

Simone heard the tremor in his voice, the rawness, knew he was battling his emotions. She'd only seen him cry once— the day Jayden and Jordan were born—and those had been tears of joy. He stood rigidly, but Simone could see the pain in his eyes, the defeat.

"I never realized that you were so miserable in our marriage…I thought we were good," he said softly, sadly. "If you want out, I won't stop you. You can have the house, the cars, the properties, whatever, but I want full custody of the boys."

Simone pried her lips apart, opened her mouth to apologize, to beg him for forgiveness, but nothing came out. The overwhelming sense of loss and sadness hit her like a one-two punch, leaving her weak, speechless.

Marcus felt himself unraveling, losing control. His face twitched like he was about to sneeze, and his breathing was shallow, labored. "I guess I need to go out and find my own hotshot attorney, huh, Simone?" The words pierced his heart, stung his pride. Marcus couldn't fathom breaking down in front of her, so he turned and stalked out of the room.

When Simone heard the door slam, her heart plunged to her knees, shattered into a million pieces like that lamp they'd knocked over while making love last week. A sharp pain stabbed her side and reverberated quickly down her spine. Simone wanted to chase Marcus down, wanted to make him listen to her, but she was shaking so hard she couldn't move.

Pull yourself together, girl. The boys will be home soon. Staggering out of the kitchen like a cheap drunk, she stumbled down the hall and climbed the stairs to the second floor. Crying never made anything better, she told herself over and over again. But when Simone walked into the master bedroom and saw the rose petals, the candlelit table, the oversize bowl of chocolate-covered strawberries and the gift box sitting on the middle of her bed, her legs gave way and she dropped to the floor, sobbing uncontrollably.

Chapter 18

God, please don't let it be time to wake up. I haven't slept yet!

The scent of strawberries sweetened the air, causing Simone's stomach to coil and clench. Disorientated, and still half-asleep, she threw off her covers and rolled onto her side. Simone felt queasy, like a cruise ship passenger who'd overeaten at the twenty-four-hour buffet, but she lifted her head off the pillow and peeled open one eye. And there, standing beside the dresser, holding an oversize plate topped with toast, cheese and fruit, were her adorable twin boys.

"Surprise!"

A smile found her lips. Wearing identical uniforms, and ear-to-ear grins, Jayden and Jordan looked so much like their father, it made Simone's heart ache. She still couldn't believe that Marcus was gone. Not after everything they'd been through. Not after five great years of marriage. Living without him was torture, by far, the worst thing that could have ever happened to her. Simone had never been the weepy type and was always in control of her emotions, but every time she looked at her sons, the tears came.

"Look, Mommy, we made breakfast!"

"I can see that." Yawning, she sat up against the headboard and stretched her arms high in the air like a yoga instructor. It was her day off, a day she'd been looking forward to spending with Marcus, but sadly, he wasn't home. Hadn't been since their argument. And like every day since he'd left, she wondered where he was and how he was doing. It had been a week since he'd walked out on her—seven lonely, miserable days—and she hadn't seen or heard from him since. No calls, no texts, no emails, no nothing. Simone wanted to work things out, but she didn't know how to bridge the gap between them. She'd called and left a message on his cell phone yesterday, but she couldn't bring herself to phone again. What if he yelled at her? Or hung up? What would she do *then?*

"Something smells delicious," Simone said, sniffing the air. "What did you boys make?"

Jayden pointed at his brother. "We wanted to make pancakes, but Jordan dropped the pancake mix on the floor, so we made fried toast instead."

"Fried toast?"

"Yeah, and we added fruit just like you do."

Simone hid a smile. "Oh, baby, you mean *French toast.*"

"That's what I said, Mommy."

"Boys, you're not allowed to use the stove by yourself, remember? It's dangerous and you could get seriously hurt."

"We know. That's why we used the toaster." Jordan swiped the fork off the plate, jabbed a strawberry and swirled it in the maple syrup. "Open up, Mom!"

Simone wasn't hungry, but although the thought of eating made her stomach lurch, she accepted the fruit offered and chewed merrily. It was the sweetest thing she'd ever tasted, something she'd never willingly eat again, but she kissed her sons and thanked them for being so thoughtful. "It's time to get cleaned up, boys. School starts in an hour, and we can't be late!"

In the bathroom, she dusted the flour off their sweaters, put on their bow ties and combed and brushed their hair.

"Mommy, is Daddy going to be okay?"

Taken aback by the question, Simone tried not to show that Jayden's question had rattled her. "Daddy's fine, baby," she said, presenting a calm, poised face.

"But yesterday when I was playing in Daddy's office I heard him tell Uncle Nate that he was going crazy without you."

Jordan piped up, "And a boy in our class said his crazy brother eats bugs and rocks!"

The boys dissolved into a fit of giggles.

"What else did your dad say?" Simone knew she was fishing for information, knew that a good mother never encouraged her children to gossip, but she couldn't help it. How else was she supposed to know what Marcus was thinking when he refused to talk to her?

"Daddy said he misses you, and that he hasn't had a good night's sleep in days."

Hope ballooned in Simone's heart. Marcus missed her?

"You have to stop tickling Daddy, though. He hates it."

Simone didn't understand, but before she could question Jayden further, Jordan explained.

"Yeah, Mom, Jayden's right. I heard Daddy tell Uncle Nate that you do things in bed that make his head spin."

Humiliation singed her cheeks, but when Jordan did a spot-on imitation of his dad—complete with the trademark grin and booming chuckle—Simone cracked up. It was the first time all week she'd had a good, hard laugh, and long after she had dropped Jayden and Jordan at school, she was still giggling about all the hilarious things they'd said.

An hour after leaving Webber Academy for Boys, Simone pulled into Glamour Girlz Beauty Salon and found the last vacant space out front. Choosing to think about how much fun she'd had that morning with her sons instead of how much she missed Marcus, she activated the alarm and hurried inside the trendy salon. Angela was the first person Simone saw when she entered the jam-packed waiting area, and when her friend waved like an overzealous crossing guard, Simone laughed out loud.

"Hey, gorgeous!" Angela greeted, giving her a tight hug. "I was just about to call you."

"Sorry I'm late. I had to drop the boys off at school."

Simone wanted to sit down, but there wasn't an empty chair in sight. Women with busted weaves, chipped nails and bushy eyebrows flipped impatiently through magazines, played on their cell phones and shot evil daggers at their respective hairstylists.

Picking up two of the complimentary sodas on the table, Angela handed one to Simone, broke the tab on her own and took a long, satisfying drink. "Um, that tastes good. I was in such a hurry to get here I didn't have time to eat breakfast."

"How was Philly?"

"Girl," Angela drawled, eyes flashlight bright, lips curved into a devilish smirk, "you wouldn't believe all the mess I uncovered on these pro athletes."

"I can imagine."

"No, trust me, you can't. They're assaulting women, betting on games *and* bribing cops. I've found so much dirt my one-hour special has become a three-part series!"

"Wow, Angela, that's great!"

"I know, huh? I'm so excited for the segment to air, I can't sleep. And you know how I feel about getting adequate beauty rest!" Angela laughed at her own joke. "I've been posting teasers on Facebook, and tweeting about it, too, and the response has been so overwhelming the station's decided to air part one on Friday instead of next month."

"I'm so happy for you. This could be the big break you've been waiting for, Angela. The one that will catapult your career to the next level."

"Let's hope so, because I'm sick of *Eye on Chicago* being at the bottom of the ratings."

"After your segment airs you'll be leading the pack!"

The women bumped soda cans. "Amen to that!"

"So, how are *you* doing?" Angela asked, taking off her jacket and draping it over her arm.

"Good. Great. Things couldn't be better."

"That must mean you and Marcus made up. When did he come back home?"

Simone stared down at her feet. Her throat was sore and it hurt to swallow, but she forced the truth out of her mouth. "He didn't."

"Do you want me to try talking to him?"

"No, that might make things worse." *He's left you and probably already hired a divorce attorney,* her conscience reminded her. *What could be worse than that?*

"I know you're sick of hearing me saying this every day, but try not to stress. You and Marcus love each other. You'll work things out."

"You think so?"

"For sure. In the meantime, keep your head up. You have your kids, your family and a great new job to be thankful for." Slanting her head to the right, she grinned. "*And* you put the *g* in *gorgeous,* girlfriend. You're working the hell out of those jeans!"

Lifting her gaze up from the floor, she raised her head and straightened her shoulders. What Jayden and Jordan told her that morning came to mind. All wasn't lost. Marcus still loved her, still desired her, that much Simone knew for sure. Two months ago, she'd done a "drive-by" on her husband, and she still remembered how much wicked fun they'd had in his office. "I should bring Marcus lunch when we finish up here. It's been ages since I did that, and maybe a warm meal will soften him up a bit."

"Now you're talking! Marcus will be so happy to see you he'll forget all about the—"

"Simone, heifer, is that you?"

Tameika, her longtime stylist with the bigger-than-life personality, rushed over. Squealing, she threw her arms around Simone and squeezed with all her might. "I haven't seen you in a minute. How the heck are you, sisterfriend?"

Simone laughed. Angela was right; coming to Glamour Girlz to get their hair and nails done was a good idea. She needed something to take her mind off Marcus, and the outrageous things Tameika said always cracked her up. "I'm good. Can't complain."

"You've been driving around the city with your hair looking like *this?*" Tameika reached out and combed flawlessly manicured fingernails through Simone's windswept locks. "You need to come in every week for a treatment or you're going to lose all this thick, healthy hair."

"I got a new job, and now that the boys are in school and taking every extracurricular activity under the sun, I'm busier than ever."

"Missed you at the mayor's luncheon yesterday," she said, popping her chewing gum. "Shoot, if my man was being honored, I'd be sitting front row in my Sunday best! I'm taking hair, makeup and a hot little number from Baby Phat!"

Simone swallowed hard and took a moment to digest this new, shocking piece of information.

And when she noticed everyone in the salon—from the wailing toddler to the plus-size manicurist with the 1970s bouffant—was staring at her, her temperature soared. "Marcus received a community service award?" she asked, unable to believe it. Not because he didn't deserve the recognition, but because he'd never said a word to her.

"He didn't tell you?" Tameika made a sucking sound with her teeth. "Shoot, he's fine *and* humble? Girl, I'd kill you and assume your identity if I thought I could get away with it!"

Everyone in the room cracked up.

"I talked to your brother-in-law, you know, the buff one with the smoky eyes. He's hot, but I just wish he had a little more paper. Everyone knows mechanics don't make no money—"

"Derek was at the luncheon?"

"Yeah, the whole family was there. Well, everyone except you."

Simone felt a laser-sharp pain in her side. It was so crippling, so debilitating, her knees buckled. Water filled her eyes as she struggled to control the trembling in her arms and legs.

Why didn't Marcus remind me about the luncheon? Or mention that he was receiving a citizenship award? The truth hit Simone like a slap in the face. *He didn't tell me because he didn't want me there.* It was as simple as that. And the realization that Marcus didn't care about her, didn't love her enough to include her, was more than she could bear.

Mumbling an apology to Angela and a promise to call her later, Simone spun on her heels and rushed through the salon and out the door before the first tear hit her cheek.

Chapter 19

"You've got this," Marcus told himself, staring at his reflection in his office mirror. "That job with the Chicago Bears is yours for the taking, so don't screw this up." Feeling his confidence grow, he adjusted his pinstripe suit jacket. He felt like his tie was strangling him, so he loosened the knot. It didn't help any. The lump in his throat and the heaviness in his chest still remained.

"How the hell did things get to this?" he asked himself, his gaze straying to the framed picture displayed proudly on the wall. The one he'd taken with Simone and the kids at the water park last summer. "How could things have gotten so screwed up so bad?"

His meeting with the general manager of the Chicago Bears was in an hour, but instead of prepping for his interview or reviewing his notes about the championship winning team, he was replaying the argument he'd had with Simone. It was all he could think of. The only thing on his mind. That and how their separation was affecting Jayden and Jordan.

Marcus stared back at his reflection. He looked sluggish, like an emergency room doctor at the end of a twelve-hour shift, and he was so tired he couldn't even smile. *That's because I have nothing to smile about,* he thought sourly, turning toward the window. A layer of low, gray clouds drifted across the sky, and the bleak, chilly weather mirrored his bitter mood.

Patting back a yawn, he returned to his desk and flopped down on his chair. He felt run-down, bummed, had zero energy. And until he made up with Simone, he could kiss a good night's sleep goodbye. Walking out on her had been the biggest mistake of his life. He should have stayed, should have tried to talk things out. Marcus was scared to death of losing Simone, and he knew if he wanted to make his marriage work, he had to make some big changes in his life. His wife needed him, and so did his sons, and he wanted to be there for them. He had to go to Simone, had to tell her that he was willing to change. He'd planned to do just that yesterday at the mayor's luncheon, but Simone was a no-show. He'd been looking forward to seeing her all week, and he'd spent the whole afternoon with his gaze fixed on the ballroom doors.

Why didn't Simone attend the luncheon? Had she been busy drawing up divorce papers with Jaxson Stafford? All kinds of terrible thoughts ran through his mind. Early on in their marriage they'd agreed never to use the *d* word, and up until now, neither one of them had.

Hanging his head in shame, he scratched at the stubble on his jaw. If he ended up losing his wife, he'd never be able to forgive himself. He couldn't, no, *wouldn't,* lose his family over this. Simone was his heart, his soul, the only woman he wanted to spend his life with.

Man up, man, *and do what's right!* Marcus raised his head and straightened his shoulders. Thanksgiving was next week, and he had no intention of spending the holiday alone. As soon as his meeting wrapped up he was going home—back to where he belonged, back to his wife and kids. His family. The people he loved more than life itself. He was prepared to do anything to make amends, because he couldn't imagine living another day without Simone. He wanted to love her, kiss her, wake up every morning with her cradled in his arms, her soft scent perfuming the air with its sweetness.

His phone rang. Hoping against all hope that it was Simone, he snatched it up off the cradle and waited to hear her sultry tone on the other end of the line.

"Hello, Mr. Young, this is Jayden and Jordan's music teacher, Ms. Watkins." Her voice was crisp, as commanding as a drill sergeant, the complete opposite of his wife's silky tone.

"Hello, how are you?"

"Not good, I'm afraid."

Marcus blew out a breath. He knew what this was about. This wasn't the first time he'd spoken to one of his son's teachers, and, sadly, he knew it wouldn't be the last. Jayden was a model student, but Jordan loved to cause trouble. He played pranks on his friends, had a hell of a time paying attention in class and loved ripping down the halls. Marcus sighed. He'd been the same way at that age, but that didn't mean he was going to excuse Jordan's behavior. He wasn't. He was going to give his son a stern talking-to—again. Marcus only hoped this time he wouldn't crack up when Jordan made that sad, puppy dog face.

"Mrs. Young hasn't arrived yet to pick up the boys, and she isn't answering her cell or your home phone, either."

Marcus frowned and checked the time on his watch. "But it's almost five o'clock. She should've been there an hour ago."

"I know, that's why I decided to call you. This is so unlike her. Mrs. Young is always the first parent to arrive, and when she didn't show up after thirty minutes, I started to worry."

"Have you tried her office?"

"Yes, apparently today's her day off."

"It is?"

His question was met with silence.

"Please, don't take offense to me asking, Mr. Young, but is everything okay at home?"

"Why?" he asked, dodging the question. "Did the boys say something?"

"No, Jayden is his usual sweet, sensitive self, and Jordan is as rambunctious as ever." She laughed, and added, "He's racing around the music room as we speak!"

Her joke lightened the mood, but Marcus's mind was spinning, racing, trying to make sense of what was going on. "I'll come and pick up the boys."

"Okay, they will be waiting for you in the front office."

"Great, thanks!"

If he hurried, he could pick up the boys and be back in time for his four o'clock meeting. After leaving a message on Simone's voice mail, he buzzed his secretary and told her he was stepping out. As he swiped his cell phone off his desk, it rang. Marcus put it to his ear, but when he heard Derek's deep, raspy voice, his first thought was to hang up.

"You still mad?"

Marcus felt the muscles in his jaw tighten. Hell, yeah, he was still mad. Because of his bigmouthed brother his marriage was in shambles. His conscience rejected the claim. *You had a hand in it, too, you Trojan workhorse!* "What do you want, Derek? Now's not a good time."

"I'm just leaving downtown. You free for a bite to eat?"

Marcus put on his leather jacket. "No. I have to grab the kids from school."

"Let's hook up later then."

"Hey, D., can you do me a favor?"

"Sure, bro, anything."

While Marcus searched for his car keys, he explained to Derek what was going on. "I'm sure it's nothing, but I just want to make sure Simone's okay, so can you stop by my place and see—"

"I can't."

"Why not? You're only a few blocks away."

"I know, but the last time I saw Simone I was a complete ass, and I don't want her to smack me!" His tone was serious, somber. "I was pissed off about getting fired from my job and took out my frustration on her."

"All will be forgiven if you swing by the house and check on her for me."

"Why can't you go? Got a big meeting you can't miss?"

Marcus winced. His brother didn't mean to offend him, but the damage had been done. His friends and family thought he was a workaholic, someone addicted to brokering deals and making money, but he wasn't. He worked to forget. To forget the explosive arguments his parents used to have, to forget all the times his father called him a stupid mistake.

Giving his head a hard shake, he obliterated all thoughts of his estranged father from his mind. He'd made it. Risen above the verbal and physical abuse and built a life that he could be proud of. A life that included a beautiful wife, two awesome children and a business that was growing in leaps and bounds.

"Why don't *I* go pick up the boys and you go check on Simone?" Derek suggested. "I'll take Jayden and Jordan back to Mom's, and you can come scoop them later."

"Thanks, D. I owe you one." Marcus heard his phone beep, knew he had another call coming through and told Derek he'd call him later. "Hello?"

"Hey, it's me, Angela."

Sighing in relief, he dropped down on his seat. "What happened? Did Simone forget to charge her cell again? Is that why she isn't answering her calls?"

"No, she's…she's in the hospital."

When Marcus shot to his feet, his chair flew across the room and banged into the wall. Head and heart pounding, he pushed the questions running through his mind up and out of his mouth. "What happened? Is she okay? Is she hurt?"

"I—I—I don't know," Angela stammered, her tone shaky, scared. "One minute we were outside the beauty salon talking, and the next thing I know Simone's doubled over in pain. The doctors think it's her appendix, but they won't know for sure until the X-rays come back."

"Can I talk to her?"

"No, the nurse gave her some painkillers that knocked her out cold."

"I'm on my way." But instead of tearing out of his office, Marcus clasped his hands and stared up at the ceiling. Then he did something he hadn't done in years: he prayed.

Chapter 20

Marcus burst through the emergency room doors of Northwestern Memorial Hospital, his heart pounding, the sleeves of his suit drenched in fear and sweat. Overrun with patients, and distraught-looking family members, the emergency department was alive with chaos and activity. Monitors beeped, strident voices argued in foreign languages and an elderly woman's deep, racking sobs almost drowned out the telephones ringing off the hook at the nurse's station.

Marcus scanned the waiting area for Angela. He found her sitting in a blue plastic chair, beside the window, rocking back and forth. "How is she?" he asked, stepping over a group of prostrate children doing a puzzle on the floor. "Any word on Simone's condition?"

"Not yet." Angela was wearing a brave face, but Marcus could tell that she'd been crying. Her cheeks were flushed, her eyes were bloodshot and she was gnawing on her bottom lip. "I'm glad you're here. Sitting here, waiting, is nerve-racking."

She hugged him, gripped his leather jacket so tight he could feel her arms shaking.

"Don't worry. Everything's going to be all right."

Angela sniffed, slowly nodded her head. "I know. I just hate hospitals. Every time I'm in one, I lose someone I love."

Marcus knew Angela was thinking about her mom and that cold winter night she'd died of a drug overdose and wondered if he was about to suffer the same fate.

Am I going to lose Simone? At the thought, his eyes filled with water and his body went numb. "Tell me again what happened, and don't leave anything out, because none of this makes sense."

Angela told Marcus everything. About the discussion at the beauty salon, about how Simone had stormed out crying and her futile attempts to calm her best friend down.

"This is all my fault. I should never have walked out on her." Marcus lowered his head and rubbed a hand across his neck. His conscience tormented him, laid the blame square on his shoulders. "I was angry and needed to get away for a while. I wasn't trying to hurt her...."

"I know. I believe you." Angela reached out and squeezed his hand. "Simone loves you, Marcus, and she'll do anything to make you happy, even read silly self-help books to improve your marriage. But when you blow Simone off for work it makes her feel like you don't care—"

"But I do!"

"Then show her."

He nodded, gave some serious thought to what she said. "I hear you. And I will."

"Don't let me down, Marcus. I'm counting on you!"

They laughed, but the tension and stress hovering over the waiting area remained.

"What's the name of Simone's doctor?" he asked, watching a group of white lab coats exit the elevator. "I need someone to tell me what's going on."

"I can't remember his name." Angela scanned the waiting

room, then pointed at a slim, brown-haired man in glasses. "There he is. He's standing right over there, in front of the computer station—"

Marcus marched over to the circular front desk and tapped the casually dressed physician on the shoulder. "Excuse me. My wife, Simone Young, was rushed here a couple hours ago, and I'd like an update on her condition."

He offered his right hand. "I'm Dr. Frederickson. Your wife is one of my patients."

"How is she doing? Do you know what's wrong?"

"Actually, I was just looking over her test results when you came over."

"And…" Marcus prompted, sucking in a deep breath.

"Your wife has an ovarian cyst trapped in her left ovary." Dr. Frederickson raised an X-ray film in the air and pointed at a gray, fuzzy clump. "It's twisted, and rather large, about the size of a kiwi. She's in excruciating pain, but for the time being she's stable."

His heart caved in his chest, then plummeted to his knees. "Is it serious?"

"If the cyst continues growing, she may need to have surgery."

"So…" Marcus paused when he a cold shiver tore down his spine. He took a moment to regroup, to channel positive thoughts, before asking, "What happens now?"

"Normally, I'd send a patient home with a prescription for a painkiller and urge them to make a follow-up appointment with their family doctor. But because your wife's still in her first trimester, I'd like to keep her for a few days of observation."

Marcus frowned. He puzzled over Dr. Frederickson's words, tried to make sense of his baffling remark. "Hold on." He shook his head, raised his hands in the air as if to stop the physician from saying anything else. "I'm sorry, what did you just say?"

"I said, normally in these situations I'd send the patient home with a prescription for—"

"No, *after* that."

The doctor gave a slight nod of his head. He wore a grin on his slender, chiseled face. "I take it you didn't know your wife was pregnant."

"She is?"

"Yes, Mr. Young, she is."

Struck dumb, Marcus stood there, his mouth agape, his eyes wide, blank pools of shock. "I—I had no idea," he stammered, spitting out the words. "Simone didn't say a word."

"There's a good chance she doesn't even know. Her HCG levels are low, so she couldn't be more than a few weeks along. I'd guess she hasn't even missed her next menstrual cycle yet."

Marcus waited for the room to stop spinning and his heart to quit skipping beats before he spoke. "I need to sit down." Feeling unsteady on his feet, like a marathon runner on the verge of collapse, he slumped against the wall. "I think I've had too much excitement for one day…."

Simone blinked, adjusting her eyes to the rays of sunshine pouring into her warm, vanilla-scented room. Glad that Marcus had arranged for her to have a private room, she snuggled deep into her blanket and stared at the sea of lavish flower arrangements crowding the windowsill.

A smile found her lips and filled her heart. Simone still couldn't believe it. The largest, most extravagant basket—the one overflowing with organic fruit, Belgian chocolates, gourmet cookies and aromatherapy candles—was from her estranged brother-in-law. Last night, Derek came to the hospital with dinner from the Skyline Grill and, after apologizing for blowing up at her, promised that it would never happen again. And Derek wasn't the only one showing the love. Gladys was being as sweet as pie, and she had baked one for her, too!

But the person who had shocked her the most was Marcus. He'd been taking care of her for the last three days. Imagine, her own chocolate Dr. McDreamy—but without the stuffy white lab coat! He helped her get dressed, brushed her hair and zipped down to the hospital gift shop to get her magazines, chips and anything else she was in the mood for. Simone couldn't remember the last time Marcus had lavished her with this much time, but she could definitely get used to it.

A sigh escaped her lips. Any day now, the fairy tale would come to a screeching halt and Marcus would resume his crazy-busy schedule. But until then, Simone was going to enjoy every minute they spent together.

Simone stroked her throat, fiddled with the necklace lying there. Marcus had given it to her yesterday, said he had spotted it while shopping with the boys last week and knew she'd love it. He was right. She did. The diamond-studded "Mom" pendant was jaw-dropping, and every time Simone touched it she thought of her boys—Jayden, Jordan *and* Marcus.

"Good morning, sleepyhead."

"Hey yourself," she greeted, stealing his favorite line. "Any word on when I'll be discharged? I've been sitting in this room for days, and I'm starting to go a little stir-crazy."

"Dr. Frederickson is doing his rounds, but he should be here soon." Marcus rested the plastic tray filled with muffins, fruit and coffee he was holding on the side table, then came over to the bed and kissed her. "How is my gorgeous, ridiculously sexy patient doing this morning?"

"Great. I feel alert and well-rested."

"You should. You've been sleeping for almost ten hours!"

"Hey, don't make fun of me," she argued, faking a pout. "I've had a very stressful week."

"You're right, baby, you have." Marcus smoothed a hand over her hair, brushed her bangs away from her face. "You gave me one hell of a scare on Wednesday."

"I didn't mean to."

"Why didn't you tell me you hadn't been feeling well?"

"Because we weren't speaking to each other," she admitted, staring down at the blue blanket Jayden had brought her from home. Simone missed the boys so much it hurt, and the second she got home she was going to shower them with hugs and kisses. "And besides, I wasn't a constant pain. It would come and go, so I figured it was just early menstrual cramps."

Marcus opened his mouth, then quickly closed it. Not yet. He was waiting for the perfect moment to tell Simone they were expecting, and although he hated keeping secrets from her, he had to make sure they were on solid ground before sharing the good news.

Sitting on the edge of the bed, he bundled Simone in his arms and brought her close to his chest. "If I had been home you wouldn't be in this hospital room right now."

"Marcus, don't. You heard Dr. Frederickson. This kind of thing happens to women all the time. Even if you'd been home, there's nothing you could have done to prevent it."

"I still should have been there. You're my wife. It's my job to take care of you."

"Quit beating yourself up. I'm fine, see?"

"*That* you are, baby. *That* you are…."

She giggled and rested her head on his shoulder. Simone wished she could freeze this moment in time. Life was perfect, Marcus was perfect. It felt good laughing and joking with Marcus again. Nothing compared to being with him and having his love. All she cared about was spending the rest of her life with her husband and kids, and she was prepared to do anything to make her marriage better, stronger—except read another self-help book!

"Baby, I owe you an apology. You were right. I never should have told Derek about the private things you told me the night you found out you were pregnant."

"You don't need to apologize. I had a terrible day at the office and made the argument with Derek bigger than what it was. I should have—"

"Don't make excuses for him, Simone. He was way out of line, and I told D. if he does it again, he'll be eating a fist sandwich!"

Surprise filled her. Her emotions must have shown on her face, because Marcus gave a curt nod of his head, said he was dead serious.

"I meant my wedding vows," he confessed, cupping her chin. "I promised to protect you, to shield you from all hurt and pain, and that's what I plan to do from here on out. I won't stand by and let anyone disrespect you, Simone. You're a queen, *my* queen, and I told Derek the next time he steps out of line, I'm taking him down."

His ultracool demeanor hid the anger he was feeling inside, but Simone heard the chilling edge in his voice, saw how the veins in his neck pulsed and throbbed. To lighten the mood, she changed the topic and playfully teased him about almost fainting on their wedding day. "Thank God that minister was in great shape, because I thought he was going to have to catch you!"

Marcus spoke with a smile. "I was so nervous that day. Scared out of my mind actually."

"The idea of being a husband and a father was terrifying, huh?"

"No, not at all."

"Then, why were you shaking like a leaf at the altar?"

"Because I was afraid I wouldn't be able to provide for you and the boys. I had sunk all my savings into Samson's, and I didn't have a plan B if the gym tanked."

Simone nodded, told him she understood.

"I wanted so much for you to be happy, for you to have everything you'd ever dreamed of. You sacrificed a lot for our family, and I was scared that one day you'd resent me because you had to give up your career."

"Did you feel pressure to marry me because I was pregnant with twins?" Simone asked, staring up at him. "Is that why you proposed while we were on vacation?"

"No. I knew you were the one by the end of our first date, but I didn't say anything because I didn't want to scare you off."

"Really? How'd you know?"

"Because I'd never had such intense feelings for anyone before."

"Right," she quipped, wearing a righteous smirk. "Us sleeping together after making out in the VIP section of that nightclub had nothing to do with it."

"No, that had *everything* to do with it." Marcus grinned, slid his hungry, predatory gaze down her physique. "You have this whole innocent, sweet, good-girl vibe going on, but you're a tigress between the sheets, and I *love* it!"

A shriek shot out of her mouth.

"Simone, you are, and will always be my heart and soul." Marcus raised her left hand and touched her diamond wedding ring with the tip of his thumb. "I couldn't have asked for a better wife or mother for my kids, and I love you very much. That's why, from here on out, we're going to work as a team. You're my soul mate, the woman made especially for me, and I plan to be married to you for a very long time, so hurry up and get better so I can take you home!"

"I'm working on it," she whispered, blinking to keep her tears at bay. It had been a long time since Marcus had made her feel this loved, this safe. He wasn't an express-his-feelings-every-day-type guy, but she was deeply moved by his confession. His words—his soft, sweet words of love and affection—soothed her troubled mind. They were going to make it. Going to spend their days and nights loving and caring for each other. And that amazing, wonderful thought made a warm glow fill Simone's body.

"I want to be the husband and father you need me to be, but I think I might need a little help to make that happen." Marcus bundled her in his arms and gathered her to his chest. "I was thinking, maybe we should go see Jaxson Stafford *together*."

Simone hid a smile. "I'd like that very much."

"Good, because I scheduled an appointment for the end of the month."

"Wow, that was fast. I'm impressed."

"You know how I am when I get an idea in my mind. I don't rest until it's done. That's why sometimes I get so wrapped up in my work I lose sight of the big picture," he confessed. "But I'm glad I have you to pull me back in line whenever I veer off course."

In spite of herself, she laughed. "Nicely put."

"Thanks, I've been working on that one all week!"

They laughed.

"We have a pretty good life, don't we?" Simone didn't wait for an answer. She didn't need her husband to tell her how good she had it. "We have two happy, healthy children, jobs we love, amazing family and friends."

"But…" he prompted, staring down at her.

"I don't mean to nag you, or get on your case about how much you work, but sometimes I don't feel like me or the kids are a priority."

"I know, and that's my fault. Nothing matters more to me than you and the boys, Simone. You have to believe that. I've been chasing wealth and success for years, to prove to myself, and my dad, that I could be successful, but it's time for me to slow down. The next few months are going to be really hectic for us, and I don't want you to be stressed out about anything."

Simone sighed in contentment.

"I have something to tell you, and it's the best surprise ever—" Marcus broke off speaking when he felt her body tense, stiffen. "What's the matter? Why do you look so scared?"

"Because the last time you said you had a surprise for me we ended up in freezing-cold Manchester!"

"That was a pretty awesome trip, wasn't it? Dining at classy restaurants, slow dancing in our cabin, making love in that stretch limo, then hours later on that bearskin rug…."

"You're right, baby, that was *some* weekend." Simone poked him in the chest with her finger. "Well, until you had to leave for Atlanta."

Dropping kisses on her cheeks and lips, he ran his hands

down her shoulders, massaging away every ache and pain. "Nothing like that will ever happen again, Simone. You have my word. From now on, we're going to work together as a team. There are going to be a lot of changes in our lives this year, and—"

"There are?"

Marcus nodded. "Yeah, we have to convert the spare bedroom into a nursery for one."

A laugh bubbled out of her lips. "Are you planning to adopt?"

"I don't need to. We're pregnant!"

Simone shook her head, laid her hands on his cheeks. Dark circles rimmed his eyes and stress lines covered his forehead. Poor thing. Her husband was so tired he was speaking gibberish. After they ate breakfast, she was sending Marcus home to get some rest, because Lord knew he needed it.

"I almost fainted when Dr. Fredrickson told me—"

"I'm not pregnant. I had my period a few weeks ago, and it was completely normal."

"Your blood work confirmed it, Simone. We're pregnant." Marcus smiled from ear to ear. "If they sold Cuban cigars in the gift shop, I'd smoke a whole box!"

"Th-th-the doctor must have made a mistake. Must have mixed up my lab results with someone," she said, tripping over her tongue, which suddenly felt too big for her mouth. "It's my body, Marcus. I think I'd know if I was pregnant."

"Dr. Frederickson told me a few days ago, but I asked him not to say anything until after I talked to you. I wanted to make sure we were good before I told you."

Marcus caressed her face, stroked her cheeks with his fingertips. "Are you all right?"

Positively stunned, Simone took a moment to gather herself, to allow the bombshell her husband had just dropped to sink in. Placing a hand on her chest didn't slow her erratic heartbeat or stop the painful drumming in her ears.

Simone fell back against the bed of pillows. She felt winded, out of breath, and her vision was so blurry she couldn't see. She waited until her head cleared and the room stopped spinning before she spoke. "Yeah, I'm okay," she answered, reuniting with her voice. "Just a little, no, a *lot* surprised!"

"I didn't want the doctor to tell you because I was worried how you'd take the news."

"Really? Why?"

"Because you said you weren't ready to have more kids."

"I'm not!" Simone took one look at Marcus's wide, blinding grin and burst out laughing. He was practically bouncing on his heels and so damn excited he couldn't stay still. "It's going to take me a couple days to wrap my head around the fact that we're pregnant, and that *you* found out first, but I'm happy, and Jayden and Jordan are going to be over the moon!"

His tender kiss set her heart ablaze. His hands stroked her back before settling around her shoulders in the sweetest embrace. Between kisses, Marcus whispered words of love, of sincere affection. He apologized for his past mistakes and promised a better life for her and the boys. "I love you so damn much," he confessed, his earnest tone wrapped in warmth and sensuality. "I love your flirty little smile, the indescribable magic in your eyes, how delicious you taste...."

Simone didn't want Marcus to ever let her go. Savoring the moment, she snuggled in close, inhaled a lungful of his scent. She heard a commotion in the room, then a loud, high-pitched shriek, and peered over her husband's shoulder. Standing in the doorway, pointing at each other, were Jayden and Jordan.

"Mommy, Jordan called me a stinky buttface!"

"No, I called you a stinky *butthead.*"

Marcus groaned. "I swear, these kids have the *worst* timing."

"Don't look at me," Simone quipped, smirking at him. "You're the one who asked for more!"

Chapter 21

Simone stood on the balcony of her oceanfront Boca Chica Resort suite, and watched the tide roll in. The sky was a stunning coral blue, the humid breeze was perfumed with the scent of salt water, and she could hear the distance sound of steel drums and cymbals. Today was the start of Carnival—a colorful, cheerful festival with music, dance and traditional costumes—and the whole resort was buzzing with excitement.

Her gaze swept across the lush, green grounds. Sun-seekers stretched out on the beach guzzling cocktails, and couples lazing in hammocks kissed under the towering palms that swayed in the wind. Golf enthusiasts, decked out in plaid caps and crisp polo shirts, zipped across the eighteen-hole course on flashy, yellow carts that had the resort's logo splashed across the side.

One week in paradise is simply not enough, Simone decided, swirling her straw around her fruit smoothie. She searched the beach for Marcus and the boys but couldn't find them. Too many people building sand castles, splashing in the ocean, flaunting their moves on high-powered Jet Skis. Being back in the Dominican Republic, after all these years—and with Jayden and Jordan in tow—was the best Valentine's Day surprise ever. And, it had been all Marcus's doing. No prodding, no cajoling, no begging on her part. She didn't even have to use the tricks she'd picked up from *A Sista's Guide to Seduction!*

Resting a hand on her stomach, Simone marveled at how much their lives had changed in the past four months. Working afternoons at Friendship House and doing community outreach with Lester "Hoops" DeWitt on Thursdays kept Simone busy, but she loved every minute of it. Her obstetrician, Dr. Whang, cautioned her not to do too much, but now that Marcus routinely worked from home, Simone had more free time than she knew what to do with.

Thinking about all of the sweet, romantic things Marcus had done for her since discovering she was pregnant made Simone smile. Her husband was a new man! He took the boys to and from school, was home every night in time for dinner and was always surprising her. Flowers, love notes and candlelit dinners were the norm now. So were their weekly date nights. But instead of dropping the kids off at Gladys's house on Friday like they usually did, Marcus had returned from work with the boys, announced they were going on a family vacation and suggested she pack a lot of sunscreen. The next morning they'd boarded a plane bound for the Dominican Republic, and had been playing and laughing and sightseeing ever since.

Simone heard the door close and glanced over her shoulder. Marcus was talking on his cell phone, but when he spotted her, he strode out onto the balcony. He kissed her cheek, then her baby bump, which caused Simone to laugh. He must have gone to the barbershop, because his hair was neatly trimmed and he smelled like aftershave. Though casually dressed in a sleeveless T-shirt, cargo shorts and sneakers, he made Simone's heart pitter-patter. It had been like that from the moment they met, and over the years her desire for him had only increased. Case in point: she had been feeling nauseated all day, but if Marcus so much as touched the sweet spot on her neck, it was on!

"I appreciate the very generous offer, but I'm afraid I can't accept the position at this time." Marcus chuckled and shook his head emphatically, though the caller couldn't see him. "No, sir, adding ten grand to the signing bonus isn't going to change my mind."

A minute later, Marcus ended his call and wrapped his arms around her. "Baby, how are you feeling?"

"Much better now that you're here."

"What are you doing on your feet? You're supposed to be resting."

"I got tired of lying around," she said, shrugging her shoulders. "We're in the Dominican Republic, Marcus. You can't expect me to stay in all day. There's so much to see and do!"

"Maybe if you feel up to it, we can take the kids to the parade later. Jordan said if I buy him one of those traditional devil costumes he'll never misbehave again!"

"Then buy him two!"

The couple laughed.

"Speaking of Jayden and Jordan, where are they?" Simone slanted her head to the right to get a better look at her husband. "Did you finally make good on your earlier threat and put them on a return flight home?"

"I tried, but my mom wouldn't pick up her phone!" He chuckled. "I dropped them off at the kids' camp so we could have a few quiet minutes alone."

Taking her hand, he led her over to the row of lounge chairs, sat her down in one and propped her feet up on his lap. He kneaded the balls of her feet, massaged the kinks and knots in her legs. "How does that feel?"

"Like heaven." Simone smiled, wiggling her toes. "You're spoiling me, Marcus. Soon I'm going to need one of your out-of-this-word foot rubs every day."

"All you have to do is ask."

"Can I get that in writing?" Simone giggled.

"I thought canceling my meeting with the Chicago Bears at the last minute would jeopardize my chances of getting the job, but the GM called and offered me the position."

Clapping, she gave a loud, shrill cheer. "The team's lucky to have you, baby. You're the perfect man for the job."

"I know, that's why I had to turn it down."

"You did? Why?" Simone remembered his earlier conversation on his cell phone and said, "You've wanted to work for the Bears for as long as I've known you."

Marcus nodded with a wry smile.

"I don't understand. It's your dream job—"

"No," he corrected, his gaze settling on her face. "It *was* my dream job. My priorities have changed, and accepting that position would put a strain on you and the boys. The job requires long hours, weekly travel and a surprisingly huge amount of paperwork."

"I'm sorry, baby. I know how much it meant to you."

"There'll be other opportunities," he told her, his voice strong, convincing. "Maybe when Jayden and Jordan are a bit older I'll apply again. Or maybe not. We'll see."

"I can't believe how casual you're being about the whole thing."

"I'm not going to let anything come between us, Simone." Marcus caressed her arms, used his fingertips to stroke her warm, supple flesh. "Baby, I live for our date nights! They're the highlight of my week!"

Moments later, they stretched out on the chaise longue and fed each other gourmet cheese and fruit. They discussed their plans for tomorrow, all of the incredible amenities at the resort and bumping into the minister who'd married them while shopping in town yesterday.

"Guess what?" Simone shrieked, clapping her hands together. "Angela scored six front-row tickets for Celine Dion's Las Vegas show!"

Marcus raised his eyebrows. "Wow, Angela must have friends in high places because I heard on the radio her shows are all sold out."

"I know! I almost fainted when I read Angela's text message," Simone said, her tone filled with excitement. "She wants to celebrate the success of her 'Athletes Behaving Badly' *exposé* and invited us girls to join her in Vegas."

"I'm happy for Angela, but trouble's definitely brewing. The players featured in her story are pissed, and Demitri Morretti, that major league baseball star, is threatening to take legal action against her and the station."

"Really? Angela didn't say anything when we spoke earlier."

"Maybe she doesn't know." Marcus shrugged a shoulder. "When is this girls-only trip?"

"We're flying out on Thursday. We'll spend a few days shopping, checking out the sights and hanging out at all of the famous celebrity hot spots. I can hardly wait!"

Marcus wore a sad face. "Baby, but I don't want you to go. I want you to stay here this weekend, and hang out with me."

"Really? Why?"

"Because weekends are for us, remember? The kids are going to Nate's, so we'll have the whole place all to ourselves. I'm going to turn off my cell, unplug the phone and romance you like never before," he promised, showering her face with soft kisses.

Simone giggled. "Hmm…I'm intrigued. What are we doing?"

"The same thing we did last Friday."

She thought hard. "But we didn't do anything. We spent the whole weekend watching movies and hanging out in bed."

"Exactly," he said, winking. "Only this time, I'm going to let you take a shower!"

His grin turned into a chuckle, and soon Simone was laughing, too.

"Watch out, woman, I have *big, big* plans for you."

"You mean for me *and* the babies." Simone sighed, stared down at her baby bump. "I still can't believe we're having another set of twins. I blame you, Marcus. I told you to stop popping those ginseng pills!"

"Hey, it's not my fault. Multiples don't run in my family. They run in *yours*."

Simone thought about Jayden and Jordan, thought about how much joy and happiness *and* trouble they caused whenever they were around. "Now that I'm midway through my pregnancy, I'm starting to get nervous. What are we going to do if we have two more boys?"

"Pray hard!" Chuckling, Marcus pulled her close, right into the crux of his chest. He kissed her cheek, nibbled on her earlobe, used his tongue to make circles along her collarbone. "You have nothing to be worried about, Simone. We're going to be fine. I promise. We have each other, our family and a love that will stand the test of time...."

Simone loved what Marcus was doing with his hands, loved what he was saying, how special he was making her feel. Her joy knew no bounds, and when he stroked her stomach and spoke quietly to the babies, she couldn't fight the emotion that swelled in her chest. Life was perfect, wonderful, better than she could have ever imagined, and once Simone hatched a plan so she could go with her girlfriends to Las Vegas next Thursday, she'd be on top of the world.

As she parted her lips to speak, her husband's mouth settled over hers in one scrumptious, passionate kiss. Tasting the sweet flavor of chocolate-covered strawberries on her lips was intoxicating, causing his desire to accelerate faster than a German sports car. Marcus wanted to flip Simone on her back and take her right then and there on the wraparound balcony, but then he remembered that his wife was six months pregnant and broke off the kiss. "I better stop before things get out of hand."

"I'm fine," she insisted, slipping a hand underneath his shirt and stroking his hard chest.

"Dr. Whang said you need to take it easy."

"She also said you should be taking care of me...."

Simone nibbled on Marcus's earlobe, and he released a deep, guttural groan.

"And there's nothing I'd rather do than make love to you."

"B-but the last time we made love you were so tired you spent the rest of the day in bed."

"I know," she conceded, hiding a smirk. "That's why *you're* going to do all the work."

A slow, easy grin exploded across Marcus's face. "Awww, sookie, sookie now!"

* * * * *

REQUEST YOUR FREE BOOKS!

2 FREE NOVELS
PLUS 2 *FREE GIFTS!*

KIMANI™
ROMANCE

Love's ultimate destination!

YES! Please send me 2 FREE Kimani™ Romance novels and my 2 FREE gifts (gifts are worth about $10). After receiving them, if I don't wish to receive any more books, I can return the shipping statement marked "cancel." If I don't cancel, I will receive 4 brand-new novels every month and be billed just $4.94 per book in the U.S. or $5.49 per book in Canada. That's a savings of at least 21% off the cover price. It's quite a bargain! Shipping and handling is just 50¢ per book in the U.S. and 75¢ per book in Canada.* I understand that accepting the 2 free books and gifts places me under no obligation to buy anything. I can always return a shipment and cancel at any time. Even if I never buy another book, the two free books and gifts are mine to keep forever.

168/368 XDN FVUK

Name	(PLEASE PRINT)	
Address		Apt. #
City	State/Prov.	Zip/Postal Code

Signature (if under 18, a parent or guardian must sign)

Mail to the Harlequin® Reader Service:
IN U.S.A.: P.O. Box 1867, Buffalo, NY 14240-1867
IN CANADA: P.O. Box 609, Fort Erie, Ontario L2A 5X3

Want to try two free books from another line?
Call 1-800-873-8635 or visit www.ReaderService.com.

KROM13

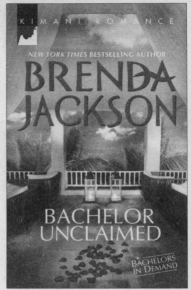